dOn't rOck the flOat

he misadventures of Willie Plummet

PAUL BUCHANAN
& ROD RANDALL

CPH
SAINT LOUIS

The Misadventures of Willie Plummet

Invasion from Planet X
Submarine Sandwiched
Anything You Can Do I Can Do Better
Ballistic Bugs
Battle of the Bands
Gold Flakes for Breakfast
Tidal Wave
Shooting Stars
Hail to the Chump
The Monopoly
Heads I Win, Tails You Loose
Ask Willie
Stuck on You
Dog Days
Brain Freeze
Friend or Foe
Don't Rock the Float
Face the Music

Cover illustration by John Ward.
Back cover photo by Ira Lippke.
Cover and interior design by Karol Bergdolt.

Scripture quotations are taken from the HOLY BIBLE, NEW INTERNATIONAL VERSION®. NIV®. Copyright ©1973, 1978, 1984 by International Bible Society. Used by permission of Zondervan Publishing House. All rights reserved.

Copyright © 2000 Rod Randall
Published by Concordia Publishing House
3558 S. Jefferson Avenue, St. Louis, MO 63118-3968
Manufactured in the United States of America

Library of Congress Cataloging-in-Publication Data

Buchanan, Paul, 1959-
    Don't rock the float / Paul Buchanan and Rod Randall.
        p. cm.— (The misadventures of Willie Plummet)
    Summary: When Willie is put in charge of the Glenfield Middle School's float for the Founder's Day Parade, he has to handle lots of conflicts and he learns to rely on God for help.
    ISBN 0-570-07125-9
    [1. Parade Floats—Fiction. 2. Gossip—Fiction. 3. Christian life—Fiction.] I. Randall, Rod, 1962- II. Title
    PZ7.B87717Dr2001
    [Fic]—dc21   00-010170

1   2   3   4   5   6   7   8   9   10   09   08   07   06   05   04   03   02   01   00

For Bruce Merrifield,
my senior pastor, mentor, and friend

Contents

①

"Got the Willies?"

Standing next to the metal shop building made me nervous. Real nervous. I knew who was in there and didn't like being so close to him. I risked a peek inside the giant sliding door. "Creep city," I muttered. I squinted and leaned closer, but it was too dark in there to see anything.

"What's the matter, Plummet?" Mitch wanted to know. "Got the willies?"

Nervous laughter. Kids fidgeted. They crossed their arms or stuffed their hands in their pockets.

"What do you think he's doing in there?" I asked.

Felix knew. "I bet he's working on that trap, getting it sharp so the first kid who messes up ... gets it!" He jabbed his fingers into the side of a kid next to him. The kid jumped a mile. More nervous laughter.

We were talking about Harvey, the school custodian. His office was in the metal shop building next to the P.E. field. It was a ways from the rest of the school, but no one minded that one bit. Harvey only had one mood. Grouch. I had never seen the trap Felix was talking about, but supposedly it looked like a giant set of jaws. Harvey kept it on the wall above his desk with a sign that read "Kid Catcher."

"Why are we doing this again?" I asked.

"Extra credit," Stacey Brittle answered. She had at least 10 pounds of books under her arm. Her short black hair flipped under and jabbed her neck. Her glasses made her big green eyes look even bigger.

"Oh yeah ... " I muttered. By helping out with the Founders' Day Parade we would each earn extra credit points for our history class. The parade is an annual event that our town of Glenfield puts on to recognize its pioneers. Businesses and civic groups get involved. So do churches and schools. The parade features marching bands, horseback riders, antique automobiles, and floats. The floats are nothing spectacular, like you'd see in the Rose Parade, but they're usually not bad—except for the one from our school.

Eighth graders head up the committee, but seventh graders can help. One of the perks is that you get to ride on the float during the parade. Crowds line the streets clapping and cheering. I could see myself now, sitting on the throne of our float, waving to my adoring public.

Then I remembered Harvey and came back to earth. He had to be the crankiest man alive—and no one was quite sure why. He was known for sabotaging floats, then griping at kids like it was their fault.

"Can you believe this year's theme?" I asked, trying to break the awkward silence. "Why dairy?"

"What's wrong with it?" Stacey wanted to know. Before I could answer, she explained that the theme was to honor the Dooper family. They opened their first dairy even before the town was incorporated. Stacey carried on about how they had grown into one of the state's largest operations and had all kinds of dairy products like ice cream, cheese, and yogurt. "I think it's a great idea for a float."

"Can't be worse than last year's," I said, giving Felix a look. I had to force myself from busting up all over again. Yesterday Felix and I joked around about how lame last year's float was.

Stacey noticed and lowered her eyebrows. "Thanks a lot, Willie. I heard what you said."

"Huh?"

"A *furniture fiasco*," Stacey repeated. "An *embarrassment* to our school. A *log cabin*?"

I interrupted. "Who said I said that?"

"Hmmm ... " Stacey brought her finger to her lips and shifted her eyes to Felix. "I wonder ... ?"

I glared at Felix, my ex-best friend.

"I thought she would laugh," Felix said. "We did."

"I worked on that float," Stacey pouted. "And my sister was the student leader."

Mitch slapped me on the back. "Ouch, Willie. Open mouth. Insert foot."

"No offense, Stacey. But you gotta admit the float looked funny." I reminded everyone how it was supposed to honor an early furniture manufacturer in Glenfield. But it didn't honor anyone. The giant dresser looked like a log cabin. The drawers were supposed to open and the kids inside would sit up and wave to everyone. But the drawers got stuck. You could hear kids yelling for help. "Let me out," I joked by pounding on Felix's back. "I'm stuck."

Everyone cracked up.

Except Stacey. "That's not funny. My sister's claustrophobic. She thought she'd never get out."

"Did she?" I asked. "Maybe she's still trapped."

More laughter.

"If she hates small spaces, why would she hide in a dresser?" Felix asked.

"To get away from Harvey," I joked. "The only thing scarier than last year's float is him." I moaned and limped after Felix, doing my best Harvey impersonation. "Is that your trash? Pick it up! No running. You good-for-nothing-kids. Get to work! Detention!"

At first everyone laughed. Then they went silent. I made more jokes to loosen things up. They just stared past me. Felix clued me in with a nod. I turned around. Harvey's huge frame filled the doorway.

"You think you're funny, huh?" Harvey growled. He wore faded denim overalls and held a black cane.

I fumbled around for something to say. "Um ..."

"What's your name?"

"W-Wi-Willie Pl-Plu-"

"Spit it out!"

"W-Willie Plummet," I quivered.

Harvey grumbled and came straight at me. He limped and leaned heavily on his cane. The group parted like minnows. Harvey used his cane to draw a line in the dirt. "On the line! Move it!"

We obeyed and stood at attention.

"I'm only going to say this once," Harvey warned. He told us that the float represented our school and it was an honor to work on it. He wouldn't put up with any goofing off. It wasn't his job to make the float, just to make sure *we* made the float. He carried on about everything involved, then finished by saying we needed a student leader. Someone who would go the extra mile. Work all hours. Coordinate work times and flower delivery. Keep in close contact with Harvey. That last requirement sent a shiver down my spine. I could tell I wasn't alone. The group looked at the sky, the dirt, the field, anywhere but at Harvey.

"Whoever wants to apply for student leader, step forward now," Harvey said. His sharp eyes moved from kid to kid, daring someone to step forward.

I closed my eyes and stood still, determined not to budge. I heard the clomp of Harvey's shoes. His breath smelled like garlic and warmed my face.

"Plummet, huh?" he grumbled.

I opened my eyes. Harvey was moving away, talking about how he didn't think I had it in me.

"I don't," I blurted out. My eyes darted from side to side. The line of kids was a full step behind me.

"Way to go, Plummet," Mitch said.

I pointed at the dirt, trying to show that I hadn't moved from the line. But kids swarmed around me, shuffling their feet to destroy the evidence.

Stacey waited her turn. "Have fun, Willie. I'll be your biggest fan." She smirked and walked away. "Next time, keep your eyes open."

Felix put his arm on my shoulder. "I think she likes you, Willie."

"Funny," I grumbled. "Thanks for selling me out. First you blab on me to Stacey, then you set me up to be the student leader."

Felix said Stacey was the first to step backward. She got the idea from her sister. "You gotta admit, you kinda deserved it after what you said."

"Me?" I complained. "You joked around too." I walked away with Felix, feeling sorry for myself.

"Plummet!" Harvey growled.

I stopped in my tracks and cowered.

"Later, Dude," Felix whispered. He hurried away.

"You've got work to do, Plummet." Harvey let out a cruel laugh and limped with his cane back through the giant sliding door of the metal shop building. From the darkness he called to me. "In here, Plummet. There's something I want to show you."

I took a deep breath.

"A Chocolate Milk Hot Tub"

The next day Felix and I sat in my living room. Somehow I survived my one-on-one time with Harvey. He grumbled the whole time and made sure I got a good look at the trap. After showing me around, he gave me a list of float requirements, then let me go.

As the student leader, I had a long to-do list. The school's flatbed trailer didn't have an engine, so we would need someone to pull our float. The flowers had to be ordered. The student council had a budget to cover some of the cost, but we had to find sponsors to make up the difference. Designing and constructing the float was also our responsibility. "This is a ton of work," I blurted out. "A *ton*!"

"Bummer, Dude," Felix said. He propped his feet on the arm of the couch and held the remote. He flipped through the channels like he didn't have a care in the world.

"Give me that!" I snatched the remote from Felix and turned off the TV. "If it wasn't for you, I wouldn't be in this mess. Thanks for telling Stacey what I said."

"It wasn't on purpose." Felix acted like he was still trying to make sense of it himself. "At first it was just Sam. But when kids heard her laughing, they came over. You should have been there. Everyone was laughing and giving me attention, like I was *the man*."

"Great. You're the man and I'm the chump."

"Don't worry," Felix assured me. "I could tell you were desperate for help, so I did some recruiting. Wait until you see who shows up today."

"*Desperate*? Since when am I desperate?"

Felix held up his hands in defense. "If you don't want my help, just say so. Besides, we have a pact and you broke it. I was just letting you suffer the consequences."

Our pact was to live by Ephesians 4:29. It was our youth pastor's idea after what happened at a recent youth meeting. We were in the hall talking when Diane Munzi walked by with the frizziest hair you've ever seen. I said to Felix, "Now you know why light sockets and fingers don't mix." He laughed and made a wise crack too. What we didn't know was that our voices traveled down the hall into the youth room. Diane heard us and rushed to the girl's room. When she came out, her eyes were red and puffy. We knew she had been crying. We felt totally guilty and apologized, but our youth pastor didn't think that was enough. He challenged us to memorize Ephesians 4:29 and hold each other accountable to live by it. That was easier said than done.

"I was just kidding about last year's float," I complained.

"Then you shouldn't have cared if Stacey heard about it," Felix told me.

We were still arguing when the doorbell rang.

"It's open!" I yelled.

Phoebe Snyder, my nine-year-old next-door neighbor came in and sat on the carpet. "Where is everyone? I thought this meeting started at four?"

I looked at Felix then back at Phoebe. "What are you doing here?"

"My friend Katie's older brother's girlfriend's cousin is friends with one of the brothers of a girl you invited. Word is you're desperate." Phoebe held up an individually wrapped slice of American cheese. "I heard you wanted us to bring dairy products. This is all my mom would give me."

After shaking my head at Felix, I pulled Phoebe to her feet. "Phoebe, no offense, but you can't help with the float."

She stood her ground. "Why not? Cheese is a dairy product. I brought what I was supposed to."

"The float from Glenfield Middle School is supposed to be made by *students* from Glenfield Middle

School. Now scoot." I lightly escorted Phoebe to the door. "Scoot! Scoot!"

Phoebe made a last stand. "Come on, Willie. I can help. I love flowers."

"Thanks anyway," I said. I closed the door and laughed. "She loves flowers alright. If I handed her a flower to put on the float, she'd keep it and tell everyone it was from me. What a nightmare!"

"You think so, huh?" Felix suggested. I could practically see the wheels turning in his head.

"You didn't hear that," I ordered.

"Hear what? The part about Phoebe being your worst nightmare?"

"That's not what I said."

"Close enough. How does Ephesians 4:29 go again? Something about, 'Let no unwholesome talk come out of your mouth, but only what is helpful for building others up according to their needs that it might benefit those who listen.'"

That was just like Felix to memorize the verse before me. He definitely had the brains for it. I was still fuming over a comeback when the doorbell rang again. This time I opened it myself.

Sam walked past me without a word. She plopped down on the recliner looking guilty. "Bad news, guys. I can't help on the float."

"Why not?" Felix asked.

"At flag practice today, we found out that we're marching in the parade. That means longer practices and more of them—especially since we're supposed to learn a new routine."

"Serious?" I said. Sam's real name is Samantha and she is one of our best friends. She's good at just about everything. Not having her on the float team would hurt.

"I can stay for the brainstorming session," Sam said. "But that's it."

Stacey arrived next carrying a cup of strawberry yogurt. She straightened me out right away. "I'm only here because you begged. Otherwise I would have quit."

"Begged?" I asked.

"Felix told me," Stacey said. She sat down next to Felix and started talking to Sam.

I glared at Felix. "Begged, huh?"

I was still adjusting to Stacey's arrival when something heavy thumped the screen door. Leonard "Crusher" Grubb stood on the porch holding a half-gallon of Rocky Road ice-cream. A ring of chocolate surrounded his lips. "Open the door already!" he barked.

Felix went over to let Crusher inside. "Hey, Crusher. What's up?"

"I better get extra credit points for this," Crusher said. "And free food." He sat down and turned to Stacey. "Plummet begged you too, huh?"

She nodded.

I stood in the doorway, thinking of all the ways I would get even with Felix. Working with Harvey would be bad enough. But Crusher, the bully of our school? I comforted myself with the fact that at least with Crusher helping on the float, no matter how bad it turned out, no one would make fun of us.

A few more kids showed up, some with dairy products, some without.

Mitch was the last to arrive. He brought a hunk of Swiss cheese. He squeezed in next to Stacey on the couch, even though there wasn't room. Stacey didn't complain either, which really surprised me.

I cleared my throat. "Thanks for coming, everyone. I just want you to know, that being picked as student leader is a dream come true." I was being sarcastic and thought everyone would catch on and laugh. But they didn't. They just stared at me like I was the least funny person on earth, which is how I felt. "But seriously," I continued, "I want to thank Stacey and Felix for making this moment possible, without them, I would be kicking back in front of the TV right now watching cartoons."

Still no laughter.

"Well, maybe we should toss out some float ideas," I went on. "Who wants to start?"

"Me," Crusher said. He put the sticky carton of Rocky Road ice cream on the coffee table. "Here's what I think, the float should be a giant bowl of ice cream. I'll sit on the edge and wave to the people while all of you dish out ice cream and feed me."

Everyone bit their cheeks to keep from busting up. They stared at me, like it was my responsibility to tell Crusher that his idea topped the all-time lame list.

I stepped lightly. "Um ... yeah ... let's keep that in mind and see what else we come up with."

"What's to see?" Crusher complained. "I've decided."

"It's not your decision to make," Stacey told him. "It's Willie's."

Crusher stared me down. "Okay, Plummet. Do you like my idea or not?"

My face started to sweat. "Well, yeah, I like it ... but ... since I asked everyone to come up with an idea, we really should hear from them."

Crusher grumbled but didn't push it any further.

I let out a breath and shifted to Stacey.

"Okay, here it goes," Stacey said. "I think we should make a giant cup of yogurt with a lid. Some of us can hide inside. At certain intervals we'll pop up and wave."

Mitch nodded with approval.

"That sounds like last year's bomb," Crusher said. "But if we go with yogurt, all of you should feed it to me."

Felix went next. He thought we should focus on the production of milk. "We can have a real cow and someone can milk it."

When Crusher suggested that he would ride the cow and wave to the people, I thought Stacey would strangle him.

Mitch's idea was for a giant Swiss cheese. "We could peek through the holes."

"Swiss cheese is cool," Crusher said. "I'll kick back on top while Sam feeds me."

"Forget it, Leonard," Stacey snapped. "No one's going to feed you anything."

Sam was quick to agree.

"Touch-ee!" Crusher complained.

"Why don't you create a barn scene and get cow costumes?" Sam suggested.

"I think we should include whipped cream," Mitch said. "Everyone likes whipped cream."

"Good idea," Felix said. "We'll make a giant can of whipped cream and spray the town. They'll love us."

"Since when do people love getting sprayed with whipped cream?" Sam asked.

"So don't waste it on the crowd," Crusher said. "Feed it to me."

From there things got out of hand. Everyone wanted his or her own way. Crusher yelled and Stacey threatened to quit. The arguing turned to shouts. I tried to calm everyone down, but no one was listening. Someone threw a pillow and knocked the almost-empty ice cream carton from the coffee table. Melted chocolate ice cream dripped on the carpet.

"Pick that up!" I said, hurrying for a paper towel. The phone rang. I grabbed the cordless on the way back to the living room. "Hello?"

"Is Orville there?" a girl asked. I could tell right off it was Clarrisa, my brother's girlfriend. I couldn't believe she liked him. Orville wasn't what you would call a ladies' man. He had bad breath, BO, and a fondness for loud bodily noises. "Orville! Phone!"

He picked up in the family room and I clicked off the cordless. Everyone kept arguing over the float. Suddenly, Orville barged into the living room. He covered the phone with his palm. "Keep it down out here! I can't hear a thing!"

That brought quick nods and plenty of them. My brother is 16 and built like a drill sergeant. He's the kind of guy you don't want on your bad side, especially if you're in junior high. He glared for another second, satisfied with our silence, then slammed the door behind him.

We sat quietly, stunned. Orville's voice carried through the wall as he continued his conversation.

"Don't tell me," Sam said. "That was his girl-friend."

I nodded.

"Don't be a wimp, Plummet," Crusher chided. He handed me the cordless phone. "Tell him off."

Sam shook her head. "Big mistake."

Crusher scoffed. "I wouldn't let my brother treat my friends like that."

I stared at the phone, then hit the *talk* button. Time to stick up for my friends. But Clarrisa's voice kept me quiet. She was singing. It sounded like a soupy love song I had heard on the radio.

Everyone snickered and covered their mouths.

I didn't know what to do. Hanging up made the most sense. But I couldn't. Clarrisa actually sounded good. The fun part would be hearing Orville's response when she was done.

At least that's what I thought.

Then we heard it.

Willie the Weasel

"Urrrrp!" Orville burped. Deep. Long. Loud. It was disgusting.

Eyes darted from person to person. Then we let loose. We roared like a studio audience. "What's so funny?" I heard Clarrisa ask.

Before I could answer—or at least hang up—the door to the family room swung open. Orville stood there, raging.

I swallowed hard and didn't make a peep. But everyone kept laughing. Some kids even applauded.

"How long were you listening?" Orville demanded.

"Urrrrp!" Crusher let out. "That long."

Orville pointed at me. "You're toast!" Fortunately, he paused to give Clarrisa an explanation of what happened. I could tell it wasn't going well. Orville's voice had a pleading tone, like when he was in trouble with Mom. He kept getting interrupted. All the while, his eyes never left me.

"Meeting adjourned," I said.

Stacey put up a fuss. "But we haven't ... "

I bolted for the front door. Normally, I would have locked myself in my room. But from the look on Orville's face, no door would stop him. I needed to escape—and fast. I crossed the front yard and sprinted down the street. I felt bad about deserting the committee, but this was a matter of life and death.

I didn't go home until dinner. By hopping fences and hiding in bushes, I managed to avoid capture. Eventually, I ended up in the supermarket and browsed through the dairy section. Stacey was right about the Dooper family. They produced all kinds of products. Yogurt. Ice cream. Cheese. They had five kinds of milk alone: Homogenized, low fat, reduced fat, non-fat, even extra rich. I was impressed, just not inspired. Even with all the choices right in front of me, I didn't come up with a good float idea.

I made sure I was the last to sit down at the dinner table. I knew Orville couldn't hurt me with Mom and Dad right there. He might land a good punch or kick under the table, but that's it. As the food was passed, I braced myself for pain. I kind of wanted it; then I wouldn't feel so guilty. But Orville didn't hit me. He just stared at his blue plate with empty eyes. His jaw muscles flexed under his skin.

"Smells great, Mom," I said, scooping brown rice on my plate. The steam warmed my face. I extended the dish to Orville.

He ignored me. His eyes never left his plate. His mouth never opened.

"Orville, you need to eat," my mom said.

"I'm not hungry." He tossed his paper napkin on the table then stomped upstairs.

My parents didn't object. That could only mean one thing. I was in trouble. Deep, deep trouble.

Amanda, my 17-year-old sister, started in on me. "Way to go, Willie. Hope it was worth it."

"Worth what?" I asked, playing dumb.

Amanda didn't fall for it. "You know what I'm talking about. Thanks to you, Clarrisa broke up with him."

"What?" I cringed.

"Can you blame her?" my mom asked.

I tried to give my side of the story. I told them we laughed at Orville's gross burp, not Clarrisa's singing. If Clarrisa broke up with Orville, it was his fault, not ours.

No one bought it. Even my mom, who would normally have a fit over bad manners, still blamed me.

"Since when is it okay to listen in on someone else's phone call?" my dad wanted to know. He pointed out that what I did was wrong and rude. "You have no right to talk about bad manners."

"But he yelled at us first! We were just getting him back."

My dad put down his fork and exchanged a disappointed look with my mom. He told me that the next time I felt I needed to "get back" at my brother, I should try forgiving him instead. "Willie, everything in life isn't a joke. You owe your brother an apology."

"And Clarrisa," my mom added.

I let out a big long sigh. "She really broke up with him?"

Amanda took a small bite of rice, then dabbed her mouth with her napkin. "She won't even speak to him. And tomorrow would have been their three-week anniversary."

I was tempted to make a joke about how ridiculous a three-week anniversary was, but decided against it. In Orville's case, the fact that he even had a girlfriend was a miracle. Besides his BO and bodily noises, he usually had grease under his fingernails from working on his truck. I was amazed that Clarrisa liked him. She was cute, intelligent, and in the high school praise band at our church.

"Amanda, maybe you should make Orville your project," I reasoned. "You know what girls like."

"No way."

"Come on," I pleaded. I promised to talk to Clarrisa and told Amanda all she had to do was help Orville with some of his rough spots.

Amanda dabbed her lips then neatly folded her napkin on the table. She said she would be willing to help Orville, but only if he asked. "I guess it couldn't hurt."

"I wish I could say the same thing," I said. Just thinking about what Orville would do made me rub my arm and chew my food a little slower.

Once I finished eating, I avoided going to my bedroom. It was upstairs next to Orville's room and I figured the longer I gave him to cool down the better. Instead, I went to the family room to call Felix. I wanted to know what happened in the committee after I left.

When Felix answered the phone, I could hear the radio in the background.

"As soon as Orville chased you out, everyone took off," Felix explained. "I think they thought what you did was kind of mean."

"*Mean*? But they were laughing." I couldn't believe the team had turned on me so quickly. It wasn't fair.

Felix talked more about what happened, but I had trouble hearing him over the radio. "Would you turn that thing down," I said.

"Can't," Felix said, raising his voice. "There's supposed to be an announcement about the Founders' Day Parade. Besides, the DJ's funny. I'm getting new material."

"Not again," I moaned.

"You should hear what the committee said about you after you left."

Before I could tell Felix I didn't want to, he told me anyway. "*Willie the weasel* came up a few times."

I twisted the phone cord into a knot. "*Willie the weasel?*"

"No offense, Dude, but I don't think you impressed anyone with your leadership skills. Maybe you should skip Ephesians 4:29 and find a verse on leadership. Right now, I don't think they'd come back if you paid them."

"Sure, that's what I'll do," I joked. "I'll pay them. I'll ask Mr. Dooper for the money. It's the least he can do." I complained about how selfish everyone had been at the meeting. "People just want their own idea." Then something occurred to me. Why not use what everyone said? "That's it! We'll have giant milk bottles, hunks of cheese, bowls of cereal, ice cream. We can even have a live cow, Felix. A live cow! What do you think?"

"Huh?" Felix replied. The DJ's zany voice and the canned laughter must have drowned me out.

"My idea," I said, getting annoyed. "What do you think?"

"Um ... sounds great. I bet most of the kids will come back. If not, others will jump at it."

"Cool," I said. I didn't think my idea was that great, but Felix perked up in a hurry.

I hung up and went into the hall, feeling better. Then I looked upstairs. Orville's open bedroom door waited for me. Time to face the music. I swallowed hard, said a prayer, then slowly raised my foot to the first step.

At nutrition break the next day, kids swarmed around Felix like ants to syrup. They hung on his every word. I watched from a distance, rubbing my arm. Orville had landed a few punches before I blurted out an apology last night. The group around Felix started to laugh. I wasn't sure if it was at one of his jokes or my float idea. I decided to play it safe and wait for the bell.

I caught up with Felix in the hall. "Well?"

"You scored," Felix told me. "Everyone wants in. They'll meet us in the metal shop building after school. We'll check out the trailer, see what we have to work with, and take it from there."

"Awesome," I said.

"Yeah," Felix agreed. "You get people laughing and they'll agree to anything."

"The DJ was that good, huh?"

"Not the DJ. You. I told them about your brother. They ate it up. But don't worry. I didn't make you look bad. I focused on the burp and the breakup."

My chin dropped. I rubbed my sore arm. "You told them about Orville? Are you crazy?"

"Dude, relax. Orville's in high school. How will he know what junior-highers are talking about?"

"Brothers and sisters, that's how." I gave Felix an earful and told him to look up a Bible verse on gossip.

Felix got defensive and said he was just passing on information. "If that's the way you feel, I won't tell you what I heard on the radio last night."

"Then don't," I said. But as we walked to class, my curiosity got the best of me. "Okay, what?"

"Forget it."

"Come on. Tell me."

Felix grinned and taunted me. He was loving this. "I know something you don't know."

I grabbed Felix by the backpack. "Just tell me."

Felix twisted away and laughed. "I'll tell you at the meeting. Just keep recruiting."

I didn't have to. Kids came up to me all day saying they wanted to help with the float. They treated me like I was the man. After school I went straight to the metal shop building. Fifty kids were already waiting. That made me feel pretty good. Harvey's dark office made me feel even better. Without him around I could focus on the fun of float building and being student leader.

The flatbed trailer made the perfect stage. I climbed up and motioned for everyone to be quiet. "First of all I want to thank you for coming today. With this many volunteers, we'll have the best float ever."

Everyone cheered and I really got into it. I raised my voice like I was running for office. "No more log-cabin furniture! No more trapped kids! The honor for best float will be ours!"

Kids clapped and raised their arms.

I had them where I wanted them. I explained my idea of making oversized and authentic looking dairy products. I also mentioned the live cow. I finished with my latest idea, an automatic ice-cream maker and scooper. We'd feed free ice-cream to the specta-tors. "If you're interested, sign up today before you leave and be here tomorrow after school."

"What about the money?" Crusher shouted.

"The what?" I said. I noticed that the cheering had stopped.

"The money!" Crusher demanded. "Patterson said Dooper Dairy would pay us."

I swallowed and looked at Felix. My ex-ex-best friend had done it again.

Blabbermouth Blues

Felix gave me a confident nod and thumbs up. "Tell them, Dude."

"Tell them what?" I whispered through clenched teeth. I leaned down and pulled Felix aside. "What's this about getting paid?"

Felix held up his hands. "I said you'd try. That's all. Just like we talked about on the phone."

It took me a second to realize what had happened. Felix was so distracted by the radio last night, he didn't realize I was joking about kids getting paid.

The crowd grew restless. They wanted answers.

A thin girl with freckles raised her hand, "How much per hour?"

"What about free ice cream?" a guy asked.

Mitch followed. "It's all-we-can-eat, right?"

"Dibbs on the yogurt," Stacey chimed in.

I waved them off. "Whoa ... hold it. No one gets paid. No one gets free ice cream. I've never even talked to Mr. Dooper."

A rumble of complaints followed.

"You're toast, Plummet!" Crusher shouted.

I backed up and talked fast. I went over my plan to use giant dairy products and a live cow. That wasn't enough.

"Get him!" Crusher ordered. His gang of thugs came at me.

I took another step back and tumbled from the trailer. I landed in some empty cardboard boxes. Shoes scuffled and stomped. Voices grumbled. Felix had done it to me again. I let out a long slow breath, closed my eyes, and waited for the inevitable.

The thumping of shoes faded. Silence.

I peeked through a slit in my eye. The metal shop was empty.

Then someone tapped me on the shoulder. "I'll still help."

I looked up. It was Phoebe.

I sat on the edge of the trailer and scraped the rust with my fingernail. Felix emerged from his hiding place. He sat a ways off where I couldn't get my hands on him.

"I know you said I couldn't help," Phoebe said. "But I heard at my school that everyone on the float committee would get big bucks and free ice cream."

"Hear that, Felix?" I pointed out. "Your gossip already traveled to the grade school."

Phoebe sat next to me and patted my shoulder. "I knew it had to be a mistake. I figured you might let me help after everyone else split."

I laughed in spite of my misery and gave her a hug. "Phoebe, you're the best. Consider yourself an honorary member of the Glenfield Middle School Founders' Day Float Committee."

Phoebe jumped around on the trailer. "Yes! Yes!" She did a cartwheel and talked about how much she liked my idea.

That made me feel better, but not good enough to let Felix off the hook. I told him his new plan of making friends by telling stories had to stop. "This is worse than when you sold candy at a discount."

"Don't blame me," Felix protested. "You said you'd pay people." He complained that my sarcasm on the phone had misled him. "Besides, I didn't promise you'd pay them. I said you'd *try.*"

I accused him of not listening, and that he cared more about having a juicy story than telling the truth. "Maybe you should think before you speak."

"Fine," Felix said, crossing his arms. "I won't tell you what I heard on the radio."

I told him I didn't care, then realized it might have something to do with the parade.

"It does," Felix admitted. He grinned because he knew he had me.

"Okay, you win," I said. "Tell me."

Felix shook his head.

"Come on."

He grinned at Phoebe but ignored me.

"Felix!"

He adjusted his glasses and hummed. Then he tapped his foot.

"Just tell me," I demanded.

"Oh, so now you want me to speak," Felix marveled. "So it's only gossip when I'm talking to someone else."

I didn't fall for it. "No way. You know the difference between gossip and news."

That got him. He nodded and filled me in. "They announced that the grand marshal for the parade will be Mr. Arnold Dooper. Stacey was right about his company. It's huge. He has operations all over the state."

"Mr. Dooper is the grand marshal?" I thought about what that could mean.

Felix explained that Mr. Dooper would ride with the mayor in the grand marshal's carriage. Not only that, our school's float would be directly behind them.

"That makes our float the center of attention." Felix eyed the flatbed trailer. "And if you ask me, you've got your work cut out for you."

"All because of you and your blabbermouth." I jumped up and went for Felix. He deserved a good headlock. Or a wet willie. He took off, laughing and talking trash about how slow I was. He made a lap around the trailer then dodged between some tool boxes.

I finally caught up with him at Harvey's office. I tackled him and we crashed through the door.

"What do you think you're doing?" Harvey growled. He sat up on the couch and turned on a light. His gray hair was flat on one side from sleeping.

Felix and I scrambled to our feet. We stood at attention, too scared to move.

Harvey yelled at us for barging in on him. He reached for his black cane.

"It was an accident," I said.

"See that?" Harvey pointed at the trap on his wall.

We quickly nodded. The rusty jaws looked big enough to catch an elephant. I didn't want to think about what they would do to my foot.

Harvey went on about how he wouldn't put up with any horseplay.

Our chins rocked up and down as we backed out the door. Harvey limped after us. The sight of the flatbed trailer set him off again. He carried on about how terrible it looked and how it would never be ready on time. "Look at it!" he snapped, pointing at the trailer. "Look at it!"

I did, believe me. I saw rust. Grease. Chipped paint. It was definitely a project. But Harvey made it sound hopeless. It was almost as if we were looking at two different things.

"Hi," Phoebe said. She emerged from behind a cart of tools and smiled real big. Her eyes sparkled. I could tell she was trying to soften up Harvey for my benefit.

No chance.

Harvey had a fit. He said she was too young to work on the float and would need a special note from her mom. Phoebe just smiled and said that was fine. Before returning to his office, Harvey shifted back to me and Felix. "One more stunt like that and you'll both get detention. Now get to work. Hurry! I'm not staying past five. Period. If you ask me this whole float thing is a big waste of time. Founders' Day Parade. Fooey." He slammed the door.

We stood there trembling.

Phoebe was the first to move. She marched straight to the trailer and scrunched her eyebrows together. "Looks okay to me. The tires can use some air, but that's easy."

I smiled and let out a long sigh. The one person I wouldn't let on the float had become my biggest helper. "Phoebe, you're the best!"

"Just don't give me flowers," she teased. "Or I'll follow you around like a love-sick puppy."

I glared at Felix.

He swallowed. "Oops."

Phoebe grabbed a piece of sandpaper and started on the rough spots. I picked up a broom just as a whistle outside caught my attention. Sam's voice followed. I pushed open the giant garage door. Sam called out orders to the girls on the flag team. They were on the field practicing and Sam seemed mad. It didn't take long to see why. Girls talked instead of paying attention. A few leaned on their flags and looked at their fingernails. Sam finally got them going, but that was even worse. Some moved faster than others. One dropped her flag. A girl with knobby knees tripped.

The team hurried from one spot to the next, doing something between a run and a walk.

"What are they doing?" I asked.

Phoebe came over. "That's a jazz run."

"Looks more like a spazz run," I said. "They're all stiff and jerky."

Felix explained that since their coach went out on maternity leave, they had hardly practiced.

A girl twirled her flag but it wrapped around her face. When she stopped, the girl behind her bumped into her. They both fell down.

"Looks like we're not the only ones in the hurt locker," I said. Suddenly, I didn't feel so bad. Then I went back inside. So much for feeling better. The trailer's rusty nails and splintered wood burst my bubble. With a committee of three we'd never finish in time. We needed help—lots of it.

I decided it was time to give the kids what they wanted, or at least try. I'd talk to Mr. Dooper. It's not every day you're asked to be the grand marshal of a parade. It made sense that he would want our float to look great. Maybe Mr. Dooper would sponsor us after all. I almost bounced my idea off Felix, then decided that until his gossip-fest ended, he was out of the loop.

Me and My Big Mouth

When I got home, Mom was in the kitchen. Dad relaxed in the recliner reading the paper. I didn't see Orville, but his truck was in the driveway so I knew he was home. I stood at the base of the stairs.

"Keep a low profile, Willie," Dad said. "You're in deep." He explained that two kids had come into the hobby store to hear Orville burp. When he wouldn't, they burped back and forth to egg him on. "I finally chased them out."

"Felix," I grumbled under my breath. I crept to my bedroom. I even shut the door *before* I turned on the light. That's when Orville pounced. He had been waiting in the closet. He had me in a headlock in no time. "You told the whole school?"

"It wasn't me," I gasped. "It was Felix."

"Same difference." Orville flicked my ears, then knuckled my head for good measure. The next thing I knew I was in the family room with a phone shoved in my face. He wanted me to call Clarrisa. "Tell her I had nothing to do with it! Now!"

Amanda appeared from behind the door and closed it. They were in on this together. Orville told me the number and I dialed. Clarrisa answered.

"Hi, this is Willie Plummet, Orville's little brother. Um ... I just wanted to say I'm sorry about us laughing. It was at Orville not you. You sounded gre—"

Click.

"Hello? Clarrisa?" I lowered the phone and backed into the corner. "She hung up on me."

Amanda spoke right up. "Of course she did. Come on, Orville. Phase two."

Before I could ask what phase two was, I figured it out.

Amanda waited at the closed family room door. When Orville didn't move, she cleared her throat and shifted her eyes at the door. "Orville?"

He clued in and rushed over. But he swung the door too far. It beaned Amanda's face.

Orville tried to blame her. "You got too close."

Amanda felt her nose to make sure it wasn't broken. "You'll never win her back at this rate."

I didn't laugh. I wanted to, but I didn't. Amanda had become Orville's make-over manager and I wasn't about to mess it up. They went to the upstairs bathroom and I followed at a safe distance. I plopped down on my bed and watched from behind my history book.

Amanda started with Orville's hair. She picked through it carefully, like it wasn't safe. "Is this grease? It's disgusting."

"It's natural," Orville said. He told her it took a few days to get it to where he liked it. "Then Mom makes me shower."

Amanda cringed. "Good for Mom." She washed Orville's hair in the sink. Then she pulled scissors and a comb from the drawer and started cutting. Orville whined, but she kept at it. When Amanda finished, Orville's hair looked better than it had in years.

The black stuff under his fingernails came next.

"Don't tell me," Amanda said. "More grease?"

Orville nodded with pride. "From my truck." He nibbled at his fingernails to clean them.

Amanda turned her face away and said "gross" a bunch of times. Then she found a nail file.

Next, it was manners. "If Clarrisa said something funny," Amanda asked, "what would you do?"

Orville slugged Amanda in the arm. "Good one."

"Ouch!" Amanda winced. "What are you doing?"

"You asked me what I'd do."

Amanda scowled and explained that girls didn't like to be hit in the arm.

"Neither do little brothers," I added from my room.

Orville ignored me and focused on Amanda. I could tell he was taking her advice to heart. She covered lots of areas. If Orville followed through on half of them, he wouldn't just be a better boyfriend, he'd be a better person. At dinner, Amanda had Orville seat her. My mom got a kick out of that one and waited for my dad to do the same thing.

"Another thing," Amanda said. "Don't talk with your mouth full."

"I vwaassnd," Orville objected. A half-chewed bite of burrito rolled from his tongue onto his plate.

Amanda closed her eyes and didn't say anything for a while. I think she was praying. After dinner I followed them to the living room. Amanda moved on to phase three, the please-take-me-back-note. She had Orville start with a poem.

"How 'bout this?" Orville started.

"You broke up with me,
Now I'm sad and alone.
If you take me back,
I won't burp on the phone."

Amanda dropped her head. Her strawberry blonde hair hid her face. I couldn't tell if she was laughing or crying. "Um ... maybe we should skip the poem idea." She wadded up the poem and tossed it in the trash. "Let's go for the direct approach—call her."

"Why? So she can hang up on me?" Orville's mood started to change. "I knew this was a big waste of time. I'll never get her back—and it's all Willie's fault."

I went back to the kitchen where it was safe. Mom and Dad were still finishing their dessert and coffee. I knew if Amanda didn't succeed, I'd pay for it. My mind raced. I had to think of something. I prayed and thought and racked my brain.

Then I got it.

"Orville, that's it!" Dad, Mom and I joined them in the family room. "Flowers!"

"Huh?"

"Flowers. Girls love them, don't they?"

"Definitely," Amanda said. Mom agreed.

I told Orville we'd be getting flowers for the float. "You can give the leftovers to Clarrisa."

He didn't buy it. "No way. What's the catch?"

"Just pull our float in the parade with your truck." I quickly added that I needed a ride to the Dooper Dairy on the outskirts of town.

Amanda thought that was a great idea.

Orville didn't, but at least he countered my offer. "Yes, to taking you to Dooper Dairy. But if the flowers don't work, you can forget the parade."

That wasn't what I was hoping for, but for now it would have to do. I headed upstairs to start memorizing Ephesians 4:29. I also wanted to look up a verse on leadership. Without God's help, I would never get through this.

Orville drove me to the Dooper Dairy on Friday. A secretary showed us into Mr. Dooper's office. He was on the phone complaining about a price. He had buzzed hair and an oval face. Pearl buttons dotted his blue cowboy shirt. After lifting a finger to indicate one minute, he motioned for us to have a seat.

Orville sat next to me with his arms crossed. He wasn't happy. Two days had passed since Amanda began her beauty treatments. He smelled like a cologne factory, had a movie star haircut, and his trimmed fingernails were milky white. But still no Clarrisa. She wouldn't have anything to do with him.

I glanced around the office, trying to stay positive. Pictures of champion dairy cows covered the walls. One had Mr. Dooper as a young man standing next to a giant black and white cow. A yellowish photo featured an old house and barn that I guessed was the original Dooper Dairy. Mr. Dooper had a family portrait on his desk. His wife had rosy cheeks and was kind of plump. His daughter was too. She looked about Phoebe's age.

Mr. Dooper hung up the phone. "Sorry 'bout that. The dairy business ain't what it used to be." He complained about prices being down and how impossible it was to make money.

"Looks like you're doing okay," I said, trying to be nice. I glanced out the window at the rows of barns and cows. Workers hurried from here to there.

"Just getting by," Mr. Dooper said. He pushed his cowboy hat back on his forehead. "Now what can I do for you boys?"

I introduced myself and told him that I was in charge of the float that would honor his family's dairy in the Founders' Day Parade. I told him Orville's truck would pull it.

"Maybe," Orville added. He kicked me so that Mr. Dooper couldn't see it.

"Why *maybe*?" Mr. Dooper wanted to know. I could tell he didn't like loose ends.

Orville mumbled an excuse about other plans. "So Willie, what did you want to ask Mr. Dooper?"

"Um ... well, as I'm sure you know, Mr. Dooper," I started, feeling nervous. "Making a float can be kind of expensive."

Mr. Dooper's face darkened. He knew where I was headed and wasn't happy about it.

I pushed ahead. "To help with the cost, our school raises funds from local businesses. And I was thinking since the float will feature your company, maybe you would consider—"

"There's always a catch ain't there?" Mr. Dooper cut in. His eyebrows dropped. "You'll honor my family just as long as I foot the bill. Is that it?"

"No. No. You don't *have* to pay. I just thought that since you'll be grand marshal and our float's in your family's honor, you'd want it to look good."

"Kinda like pay now or pay later. Hmpf! That sounds like blackmail to me."

Orville grinned. He was loving this.

"Blackmail?" I choked. "No way!" I shared my idea for the float and explained why we needed help. I talked about the mix-up at my house and how everyone quit. I told him that everyone came back then quit again when they realized they weren't getting paid.

"Paid?" Mr. Dooper growled. "Now you want me to *pay* kids to make a float?"

"No. That's not it. I promise!" I shook my head until it rattled. My face turned as red as my hair.

Mr. Dooper grumbled some more then quieted down. He patted his round belly. "Over-sized products, huh? Would our labels be on them?"

"Um ... sure," I said. "Makes sense."

He scratched his face. "Nope. I don't like it."

I sunk down in the chair, defeated. Orville didn't even razz me.

"Unless ... " Mr. Dooper started. "Turns out there ain't enough room in the carriage for my daughter, Debra, what with the mayor and the wives and all. How 'bout if she rides on the float with you?"

I hesitated. "Um ... I guess ... maybe."

Mr. Dooper didn't give up. "You said you wanted a live cow, right? Debra could handle her, even milk her if you want."

I thought about the float guidelines. They didn't say the kids *had* to be from our school. "Okay, sure. Debra's in."

Mr. Dooper stood up. "In that case, Partner, you got a deal." His big hand swallowed mine. He agreed to provide flowers and dairy products, but stopped short of agreeing to pay anyone. "Let me go get Debra so you can meet her. She'll be a happy gal."

Orville laughed and elbowed me. "Have fun."

"Huh?"

"Look at the picture of his daughter. She's younger than Phoebe. She'll follow you around like a love-sick teenybopper. She's probably a spoiled brat, too. Now I'm really out. Don't even—"

Orville stopped. His chin nearly hit the floor.

Mr. Dooper had returned with his daughter. The picture of her was obviously taken years ago. Now she was a teenager—and cute. She had blue eyes, red lips, and delicate skin. A pink ribbon held her hair.

Orville stood so fast I thought his head would hit the ceiling. He even pulled me up. Amanda would have been proud.

"Boys, this is my daughter, Debra," Mr. Dooper said. "She loves the idea."

"I do?" Debra looked at her dad.

"Now Pumpkin, be nice." Mr. Dooper's tough-as-nails attitude had vanished. But his daughter made up for it.

"Why can't I ride in the grand marshal's carriage?" she complained.

Mr. Dooper delicately reminded her that that wasn't possible. Then he introduced me as the kid in charge.

"And I'll be pulling the float with my truck," Orville added.

"I thought you had plans," I said.

Another kick in the shin.

Mr. Dooper explained that his daughter went to a private high school in Ashland.

Orville winked and gently took her hand in his. "I guess that explains why we've never met."

"I guess so," she said, pulling away. She made it clear that riding on the float didn't mean she would help build it. "That's not a problem, is it?"

I started to get uneasy. "Well—"

"Of course not," Orville cut in. "I'll cover for you. No problem."

Debra offered a coy smile. "You will?"

"You will?" I questioned, looking at Orville.

Another kick.

Orville stuck out his chest and made his voice deep. "Sure. Be glad to."

Debra beamed with her pearly whites and I thought Orville would melt. I'd have to take him home in a bucket. Debra said she would stop by when she could, but no promises. Mr. Dooper told me to send all purchase orders his way. He'd take care of everything. He even gave us three free gallons of chocolate ice cream as we left. Driving away, I felt good, but guarded. We had a sponsor, but something about Debra and Orville made me nervous. Real nervous.

6

Clarrisa's Surprise

At church on Sunday, I hoped out of the car and hurried across the parking lot to meet up with Felix. Sometimes we sat with our families, but most of the time the youth sat together in the second row. Being up front made it easier to get into the worship service.

"Felix, wait up," I called out.

He didn't slow down or glance back. I repeated myself but he hurried through the heavy wood door of the sanctuary. I caught him just as he headed down the aisle.

"What's wrong?" I asked, grabbing his arm.

Felix twisted free. "Nothing."

"Yes there is. What's up?"

Felix moved to the side so people could pass. "Thanks for taking me to Dooper Dairy. I thought we were in this together."

"We are," I told him. "It's just that I didn't think there was any reason for you to go."

Felix didn't buy it. "You didn't want me to go."

I admitted that he had a problem with gossip and I didn't want another mix up.

"In that case, I quit," Felix sat on the end of a pew next to his family where there wasn't room for me. I tried to tell him that Mr. Dooper said yes but he wouldn't listen and the service was about to start.

Good thing I was in church. If I ever needed time with the Lord, it was now. I walked to the second row and sat down next to Sam. After a short welcome, the worship leader led us in singing. Gradually, I began to feel better. The surround-sound definitely helped. Voices lifted on all sides giving praise to God. A feeling of peace came over me. My skin tingled. The more I sang about God's love, the more I felt it.

When the sermon came, the pastor talked about Nehemiah and how the Jewish people rebuilt the wall around Jerusalem. They faced all kinds of obstacles, but the Lord helped them. He would help me too. I just didn't know how or when.

Then the service ended and I found out.

Clarrisa tapped me on the shoulder. She thanked me for calling the other night and apologized for hanging up. She brought up the float. "I hear you're having problems getting workers."

"Yeah, it's been tough."

"In that case, I want to help."

I nodded but didn't say a thing. I just stood there with a dopey look on my face thinking the Lord works in mysterious ways.

When I arrived at the metal shop building after school on Monday, I didn't know what to expect. I had spent the day recruiting, but no one would promise to help. Even the offer of free ice cream wasn't enough. Felix had told them that I ditched him and that was no way to treat a best friend. Thanks to him I was the least popular guy in school. I tried to straighten things out, but he acted like I didn't exist.

Crusher shot me down too. "First, you want our ideas, then they're stupid. Next, we're getting paid, then we're not."

Mitch was the nicest of the bunch, but he wouldn't commit to showing up until he found out what Stacey was doing.

I walked around on top of the flatbed trailer. I tried to picture it as something other than gray boards and rusty steel. But I couldn't.

"It won't build itself," a young girl's voice told me. "Let's get busy."

Phoebe walked through the sliding metal door. An entire school of junior-highers, and my only recruit was a nine-year-old girl. She walked up to the roll of chicken wire and wood that Mr. Dooper had delivered. "You scored!"

I just smiled and watched her. Phoebe could be a pest and sometimes embarrass me big time, but she was a true friend.

She noticed me smiling and got on me for not helping her. "Don't think I'm building this alone. Even I don't like you that much."

I jumped down from the trailer and explained my plan to Phoebe. We'd build the frames for the giant dairy products with wood. We'd cover the frames with chicken wire. Then we'd cover the chicken wire with strips of newspaper dipped in starch. Once the newspaper dried, we would glue on the flowers. Nothing to it.

"Before we start, let's pray," I suggested. I told Phoebe about Nehemiah leading a small group of people to rebuild the wall around Jerusalem in 52 days. "If they could do that with God's help, why can't we build a float?"

"We can," Phoebe said.

We closed our eyes and prayed. We asked God to be with us and help us accomplish the impossible. When we opened our eyes, Clarrisa was standing there.

"Sorry I'm late," she said, "but I'm ready to work."

We told her no problem and that she was an answer to prayer. We got busy on a giant milk bottle. Building the frame wasn't too bad, but shaping the chicken wire was harder than I thought.

"What's with the bowling pin?" a voice asked from the doorway. It was Stacey. "So much for the dairy theme?"

"It's a giant milk bottle," I told her.

Mitch followed her in. He pretended he was bowling. "Strike!"

Crusher came next. "You're hurting, Plummet. Good thing we're here."

They eyed our project then picked up boards of their own. In no time we were dividing up projects. Crusher and Mitch would work on the fence for the cow. Phoebe and Clarrisa would start on a six-foot block of Swiss cheese. Stacey opted for a giant tub of fruit yogurt.

"What made you decide to come?" I asked.

"Ice cream," Crusher said. "Where is it?"

I told him that Orville would bring it later.

"Orville?" Stacey questioned. She shifted her eyes at Clarrisa.

"Um ... yeah," I said, sensing the awkwardness. "Ice cream for a job well done."

Two hours later I had my doubts about the "well done" part. The Swiss cheese looked like a giant sponge. The milk bottle leaned to the right. And Stacey's cup of yogurt resembled an aluminum can. I started thinking even the most beautiful flowers on earth wouldn't help us.

But there was someone who could. Harvey.

He sat behind his desk reading the newspaper. His office door was open so he could keep an eye on us. Every now and then he checked to make sure we hadn't broken anything or smashed our fingers. He seemed as grouchy as ever.

I wandered to his door with my hands in my pockets. "Harvey, we're having a little trouble with our float."

"A little trouble?" he grumbled. He didn't look up from his paper.

I told him our dairy products didn't look so dairy.

"How do you know what they're supposed to look like?" Harvey growled.

I knew what he was getting at. "Orville was supposed to bring samples, but he's not here yet."

Harvey put down his paper and muttered something about "kids" and "irresponsible." He limped to an ancient refrigerator and opened the door. "Well, get over here." He piled me up with a milk bottle, block of Swiss cheese, and a cup of yogurt. He grabbed a can of whipped cream and a cube of butter.

"Did you buy all these for us?" I asked.

"Do you want to work or do you want to talk?" he barked, limping past me. He made his way to the work area by the float. I followed with the dairy products.

Harvey started with Mitch and Crusher. He used the claw of the hammer to remove a nail that held a crooked board. He showed them where it belonged and pointed out what else they needed to do. When he got done with them, he moved to the giant milk bottle. He looked back and forth between the real thing and the giant replica.

He shook his head, disgusted. "The neck's too thin. Your angle's way off. Looks like a bowling pin."

"I told you," Stacey said.

Harvey worked the chicken wire for a few minutes, grumbling at anyone who would listen. "There."

"Thanks," Phoebe said. She smiled like an angel and patted his arm.

I think that got to him, but he didn't show it. Still grumbling, he went back to his paper. He acted like he wasn't watching, but when someone did something wrong, he barked a few orders from his desk.

"He doesn't have to be so mean about it," Clarrisa said softly.

I felt the same way and wondered what made Harvey so grouchy. If anyone could find out, it was Felix. He loved playing detective. And the way he was swapping stories lately, he could get information out of anyone. But he wasn't here, and even if he was, I couldn't risk asking him to get involved. If he started gossiping about Harvey, we'd really be in trouble.

We were finishing for the day when Orville finally arrived with the ice cream. He had on a clean white shirt and khaki pants. He stood awkwardly away from Clarrisa and kept looking around.

Phoebe didn't even ask Harvey if he wanted ice cream. She just took him a bowl. "Here you go."

"I don't want any," he grumbled.

That didn't faze Phoebe. "Come on. It's really good. Dooper Dairy donated it."

"Dooper Dairy. Hmpf." Harvey eyed the bowl. "What flavor is it?"

"Chocolate."

He muttered and shook his head, but eventually picked up the plastic spoon and bowl. I noticed we were all watching him. Phoebe returned to lots of pats on the back. We couldn't prove it, but something told us that in her own innocent way Phoebe had just made the most miserable man on earth feel a little better.

While everyone ate, Orville pulled me aside. "Is Debra here?"

I shook my head while shoving in another mouthful of Dooper ice cream.

Orville's shoulders dropped. He looked at himself like he had dressed up for nothing.

When we finished for the day, Sam was still shouting orders at the drill team. She threatened that they would stay until dark if the girls didn't get it together. I was standing between Orville and Clarrisa, which felt really weird. They hadn't said a word to each other. Everyone else had gone home.

"Choke city," Orville said softly.

A girl had twirled her flag too fast and dropped it. When she picked it up, the pole tripped Sam.

A girl further back stopped in her tracks. "Come on," Sam complained. "It's not that hard. Concentrate."

Pretty soon it seemed like everyone was yelling at everyone. The parent who was filling in for the coach tried to quiet them but couldn't.

Clarrisa took a few steps forward. Then without a word she jogged to the group. The parent recognized her and gave her a hug.

"Was Clarrisa on the flag team?" I asked.

Orville looked on, surprised. "I guess so."

Clarrisa was introduced to the group. She offered a friendly wave to the girls, then demonstrated the proper way to twirl a flag. She threw it in the air. The flag made a double rotation before Clarrisa caught it. She repeated the move step by step with perfect precision. Girls watched in awe, impressed and encouraged. When they started again, Clarrisa ran from girl to girl, giving them encouragement and pointers.

"She's amazing," I observed. "No wonder she doesn't want you back."

"You mean I don't want *her* back," Orville said in a huff. He flexed his muscles and smoothed back his hair. Amanda's finishing school had transformed him. His clothes weren't just clean, they were in style. Forget about BO. Orville smelled even better than he looked. Too bad it had gone to his head. "I'm moving up. Debra Dooper will be mine."

"Debra? What about Clarrisa?"

"She dumped me. Forget her."

I couldn't believe my older brother. I knew he still cared about Clarrisa. And it was obvious that she still liked him. Why were they being so stubborn? That made me think of Felix. He had made a mistake, but so had I. He was my best friend. It was time to straighten things out.

The Dooper Scooper 2000

I had Orville drop me by Felix's on the way home. Mr. Patterson pointed me down the hall. Felix's door was closed so I knocked. As soon as he saw me, he raised his Bible to hide his face.

I got right to the point. "Felix, I'm sorry I didn't ask you to go to Dooper Dairy."

Felix turned a page without answering.

"I should have told you what was bugging me. It's just that you were gossiping about everything you heard and—"

Felix interrupted. "Did you come to say you were sorry or get mad at me all over again."

I held my tongue. "You're right. I'm sorry. That's all I wanted to say."

Felix lowered the Bible. I could tell he wanted to talk. He brought up what happened and how things got out of control. "It was weird. Kids would come to me just to hear the latest rumors. I couldn't believe it.

They acted like I was the man. By the time I realized how much I was gossiping, it was too late."

We talked for a few more minutes. He told me he had memorized a verse on gossip and asked me to test him. "A gossip betrays a confidence; so avoid a man who talks too much. Proverbs 20:19."

"Perfect," I said.

Felix asked me to hold him accountable to it.

"Deal," I said. "Does this mean you'll rejoin the float team?"

He nodded and wanted to hear about our progress. I gave him an update and asked him to be in charge of ordering flowers. He would need to make a list of everything we needed. That would mean talking to the kids in charge of each giant diary product.

"You can talk to everyone without causing any harm," I said.

Felix beamed. "It's about time."

Felix spent the next week coming up with a list of flowers we needed. That was the good news. The bad news was he started asking teachers about Harvey. Felix felt that we couldn't help him unless we understood him. To me it had gossip written all over it. But Felix assured me otherwise. The teachers said Harvey had always been irritable, especially when the parade came around. They guessed something happened when he was younger. But Harvey was nearly 70 and none of our teachers were around back then.

Once the wire frames were finished on each of the giant dairy products, we applied newspaper strips and starch. When that dried, we painted it. Thanks to everyone's hard work and Harvey's advice, the float really shaped up. The next step was gluing on the flowers. But that wouldn't happen until the day before the parade. With a week to go, we worked on other projects that would really make our float special.

One was the giant cup of yogurt. Stacey was going to pop out of the cup and wave. After last year, I couldn't believe it. But I think she wanted to prove she could successfully pop out of something. Mitch even agreed to pop out of the cup with her. She would wear a hat that resembled a strawberry, and Mitch would wear one that looked like a blueberry. Unfortunately, on the day Stacey needed someone to model the blueberry, Mitch was home sick.

The rest of us had gathered in the metal shop building to work on the float.

"Orville, will you model this for me?" Stacey asked.

"You bet," Orville said.

I couldn't believe it. Amanda's finishing school had really paid off. Orville even agreed to paint his nose blue. The blueberry head was an old scuba diving hood. The neoprene was thick and stiff. What's worse, Orville's head was a size too big.

"Hurry up," Orville said. "It's squeezing my brains out."

"That won't take long," I said.

Felix cleared his throat. "Ephesians 4:29."

Stacey walked around, examining the blueberry. "Very nice. I like it."

Orville started to remove the hood but Stacey smacked his hands away.

"Careful, you'll smear the paint." She lifted from the inside of the hood but it wouldn't clear his chin. Orville grimaced and made a squeaking sound. When Felix got hold and pulled on it, Orville's neck stretched an inch.

Before I could make another wisecrack, the phone rang. Harvey yelled that it was Debra Dooper. She was coming over with more ice cream. She also had something she wanted to talk about.

"Debra Dooper?" Orville gasped. "Coming here?" He went at the hood like a mad man. "Cut it off. Quick!"

"No way. You'll ruin it," Stacey complained. She sent me for help.

I came back with a crowbar.

Orville flipped. "Get that thing away from me."

"Come on, Bro. No pain no gain." I attempted to slide the crowbar under the hood, but he had a cow.

Everyone else started in with ideas.

"Try shooting grease in there," Crusher said.

I told them Orville's hair had enough grease in it already.

"It's mousse," Orville said. "The expensive stuff."

"It's your fault for having such a big head," Stacey said.

Finally, I went for Harvey. He came out grumbling and complaining. After a quick look at the problem, he grabbed the hood under each ear and lifted. It came off with a *pop*.

Just then Debra walked in. She made a face at Orville. "What happened to you?"

Orville's hair looked like it had gone ten rounds with a blender—and lost. What's worse, the blue paint on his nose had smeared all over. He was a sight.

Debra rolled her eyes then shifted her attention to me. Orville ran for the bathroom.

Debra handed over a couple gallons of ice cream then told us she needed to see where the cow would ride. She climbed on the flatbed trailer and jumped up and down. Then she patted the wood fence. "It should work. But we can't wait until the day of the float to find out."

I wondered what she was getting at. Debra noticed the oversized dairy objects. She made a face.

"Wait until we attach the flowers," I quickly added. "They'll look great."

"Let's hope so." Debra climbed down and addressed us. "I talked to my dad and he thinks the dairy cow should spend some time on the float before the parade day."

"You're not bringing a cow in here," Harvey snapped.

Debra shrugged. "In that case you'll have to finish the float at the dairy. But you'll have to arrange for rides each day."

"We can do it," I said. "I'm sure Orville will help."

"My mom might," Clarrisa said. She had just come in from the side door.

Harvey grumbled some more. "Well, maybe we can figure out a way to keep the cow here. But only for a day or so." He told me he'd look into it.

"Whatever," Debra said. "Just let my dad know." She eyed the float again, frowned, then left.

Just then Orville rushed from the bathroom. He had restyled his hair. His face was sparkling clean. "Where's Debra?" he asked in a huff.

"She's gone," I said.

"Yeah," Clarrisa added, crossing her arms. "She's gone."

The color drained from Orville's face. "Oops." He reached for the two containers I was holding. "Ice cream anyone?"

No one said a word.

A few days later I went to the lab after school to work on my latest invention, the Dooper Scooper 2000. It was an automatic ice cream scooper that would make our float go down in Glenfield history. *The lab* was what we called the back room of my family's hobby store. With all kinds of spare parts lying around, it was the perfect place for inventing. I decided on a remote control model crane to use as the arm. Buckets of ice cream would sit beside it. The goal was for Dooper Scooper 2000 to dig, lift, pivot, and drop in one smooth motion. Cones would glide by on a conveyor belt. After a scoop of ice cream dropped in each one, we would grab the cones from the belt and pass them to the crowd. Easy enough.

Felix and I worked together. He had a knack for mechanical details. Sometimes he would rely on math formulas. Other times he'd just figure things out by staring at a problem for a while and adjusting his glasses.

This time he relied on both.

"We need a lower gear in the arm of the crane," Felix said. He made a few calculations. "That will give us more torque and less speed."

"Whatever you say, Champ."

I worked on the belt and cone holders. The motor from an old electric mixer turned a long white belt of canvas. Small paper cups served as cone holders. We glued the cups to the canvas and around they went.

I eyed the belt speed. "Perfect."

Felix positioned a gallon tub of ice cream next to where the scoop would dig. "Let's try it."

I turned the electric mixer on low. The belt started to turn. The paper cups glided along, over then under. I opened a box of cones and pulled apart the clear plastic bag that kept them fresh. I started to load the cups at the back of the belt.

Felix hit the power button on the crane. It rose up, pivoted, then lowered the scoop in the ice cream. The motor strained.

"It's working," I said.

Felix grinned with confidence. "Of course."

The scoop dug into the ice cream, then started to turn. That's when it struggled. The motor slowed and make a weird whining sound.

"I think the motor's going to overheat," I said.

"Just give it a second," Felix told me.

He was right—sort of. The scoop completed the turn. But it had too much force behind it. When it broke free, it became a catapult. The ball of ice cream launched over our heads and landed 10 feet away.

Felix tightened his chin. "Not bad for a first try."

I didn't argue. Considering some of our other experiments, we were doing just fine. Felix adjusted the gears while I cleaned up the ice cream.

That's when Sam walked in. She looked at the Dooper Scooper 2000 then at me on the floor with a paper towel. "This I've got to see."

Felix gave her an overview of what had happened. She was impressed. "If only my flag team
could do that well after a hundred tries."

"Still bad, huh?" I asked. I finished with the clean-
up then joined Felix and Sam at the Dooper Scooper
2000.

"It's tough with our coach gone," Sam complained. "But still, we've been together all year! We
should have it by now—especially with Clarrisa helping us. I don't know what their problem is." Sam
guessed that maybe the routine was too difficult. Or
maybe the pressure of thousands of spectators was
getting to them. "Why can't they just get it?"

Felix and I exchanged a look but didn't say anything.

Sam noticed. "What? Tell me."

We used the Dooper Scooper 2000 as a diversion.
I loaded cones in the cups. Felix adjusted gears.

Sam didn't let up. "Tell me. What?"

I decided to say something. "It seems like you
really come down on them."

Sam put her hands on her hips. "Look who's talking. You're the one who puts everyone down."

"Yeah, but—"

"You should see them," Sam went on. "They drop
flags. Get out of position. Lose their timing. Forget
about synchronization."

I shrugged and kept loading cones. "It just seems
like you could find something positive to say."

"Yeah," Felix added. "Everyone can't be like you, Sam."

I couldn't believe Felix said that. But for a guy who liked to talk, I shouldn't have been surprised.

"What's that supposed to mean?"

"You're athletic," Felix explained. "Stuff comes easy for you."

He was right. Sam excelled at everything she tried. Softball, flags, sports of all kinds. She was smart, coordinated, talented. You name it. But it's not like she was a snob. She just accepted her abilities as the way she was. But in this case, that was the problem. What came natural for her didn't for some of the other girls on her team.

I told her some of what I was thinking.

"I can be positive." Sam crossed her arms. She didn't admit that she had been too tough on the girls, but I could tell she was thinking about it.

"Ready for test two," Felix said.

I turned on the belt then moved back to the spot across the lab where the first scoop had landed.

"What are you doing over there?" Sam asked.

"You'll see," I said.

Felix gave Sam a wink and turned on the crane.

The Dooper Scooper 2000 launched the ice cream ball over my head.

A few quick adjustments later, Felix tried again. The ice cream shot toward the first spot. I lunged with the cone. "Got it!"

"Cool," Sam said. She grabbed a cone and joined me.

Felix kept adjusting. The Dooper Scooper 2000 tossed like an automatic pitching machine.

"Watch this," I said. Instead of using my cone, I caught a flying scoopful with my mouth. Sam went for one too. Then Felix came over. We bumped into each other, catching scoops and laughing. One hit me in the eye. Sam speared one with her nose.

"I got it," Felix called out. He scrambled back and forth. The scoop of ice cream lobbed toward the ceiling. Felix tipped his head way back. He opened his mouth. *Plop!* Felix misjudged the angle. The ice cream slid down his neck and under his shirt. "C-Cold! Cold!" Felix sputtered. He hopped around like a frog on ice.

Sam and I fell over each other in hysterics.

Then Orville came into the lab wearing his Sunday best. He had promised to take us to Dooper Dairy to learn to milk Elsie and impress Debra. He wore a pressed white shirt and gray slacks. His black shoes were polished till they sparkled. "What's going on?" he asked.

He found out soon enough. A chocolate ice cream ball flew over our heads and pegged his white shirt. Then it skidded. The brown streak angled from his heart down his side.

Orville acted like he had been shot. He pointed at me, his face screwed tight. "You're toast!"

I ran around the lab table. Felix and Sam followed. Orville came after us. But his dress shoes were no match for the slick floor covered with ice cream. He slipped to one knee. More dairy bombs kept coming. It was like playing tag in a chocolate hail storm.

"Incoming," Felix shouted.

We ran around the lab dodging ice cream balls and Orville. Sam and Felix laughed and ran interference for me. About the time Orville closed in, I did what any quick thinking little brother would do—I ran to my dad.

"Dad, Orville's after me!" I rushed to the front of the store and hid behind him.

My dad held back Orville and got the story.

"Sounds like an accident to me," my dad decided. He told Orville to calm down then shifted to me. "I want the lab cleaned up before you and your friends go to the dairy."

"What dairy?" Orville said. "I'm not taking them."

"Since when?" I asked.

"Since this," Orville whined. He pointed at the stain on his shirt.

I rolled my eyes, frustrated. In the past Orville wouldn't have cared if the ice cream was stuck to his shirt and smeared all over his face. Now he wouldn't even go near a cute girl unless he looked perfect.

"Come on, Orville," I begged. "This could be your chance to get to know Debra."

"Not like this," he said. He stared at his shirt and thought about what I said. "Well, maybe if the stain comes out."

By the time we arrived at Dooper Dairy the office was closed. Mr. Dooper had left for the day, but one of the workers said Debra had asked about us and was somewhere around. He went to find her. While we waited, we breathed through our mouths to avoid the stench of too many cows and not enough air. Felix had come along, but Sam had too much homework.

When Debra finally arrived, she had on faded jeans and a red flannel shirt. She smirked at Orville. "Where are you going?"

Orville mustered a goofy Mr. Smooth smile. "Right here, Babe."

I looked around for a bucket to gag in.

"All I do is supervise," Orville went on. His voice sounded deeper than normal. "These dweebs do the milking."

"Right," Debra said. Her eyes lingered on Orville and I thought he would go into orbit. He started to shove us, then quickly dropped his arm to his side. He was trying to hide the dark spot where he had tried to wash off the ice cream.

"Something wrong?" Debra asked.

"Uh ... no," Orville said. He kept his arm against his ribs. "Old football injury."

Debra looked at me and Felix like we should give her the real story. I just rolled my eyes. She led us through some modern buildings to an old fashioned barn. It was red with white trim and had wide doors. She told us it was part of the original homestead. Loose straw and hay bales covered the floor. Orville danced around, making sure he didn't step in any-thing that might mess up his shiny black shoes. Debra glanced at him and snickered. A black and white cow waited in a stall of gray boards. The cow munched on something in a bucket, then turned to check us out.

"This is Elsie," Debra told us. She climbed into the stall and patted the cow on the back. "We use Elsie for demonstrations. She's used to lots of people handling her." Debra explained that children, teachers, and church groups had all tried their hand at milking. "She's totally tame. Anyone can milk her."

I started to feel a little relief. With that much experience, maybe Elsie could milk herself.

Orville moved to the front of the stall and tickled Elsie's chin. "Who loves ya, Babe?"

Elsie let out a sneeze. It was so strong, she stepped a few times to steady herself.

"I think she's allergic to your cologne," Debra said.

"As long as you're not," Orville gushed.

Debra turned away at that. I guessed it was to cover her mouth so she wouldn't gag. But Orville seemed to think he had really impressed her. He looked at me and grinned like he was the man. In the meantime, Elsie sneezed again.

Orville leaned on the rail next to Elsie. "Easy, little mama."

When Elsie sneezed for the third time, Orville caught on and moved away.

"Who wants to go first?" Debra asked.

Since Orville had to keep his distance, it was between me and Felix. Naturally, Felix volunteered me. "Looks like a job for the student leader," he announced.

Debra sat on a stool beside Elsie and positioned a bucket between her knees. She told me what was involved in milking and showed me at the same time. The teats were the part of the udder that looked like fingers on rubber gloves. "Squeeze with your thumb and index finger, then follow with the rest of your hand. Do the same with the other hand. Back and forth. Back and forth." Streams of milk shot into the bucket. "Got it?"

I shrugged. "I guess."

I sat on the stool and stared at Elsie's udder. It looked way too full, like a balloon that gets one too many puffs and explodes in your face.

"Go ahead," Debra said. "Elsie's about to burst."

I squeezed like she told me to, but nothing happened. "I think the milk went up instead of down."

"He's a natural, all right," Orville joked.

Debra was about to help me when a guy came in saying there was a phone call for her. She told me to keep at it, then left.

I did, but didn't get any better.

That's when Elsie got an attitude. She whipped her tail around and flicked my head. Then she stepped on my foot.

"Yeouch!" I squealed.

"Come on, Ace," Orville said. "You're making us look bad."

"Then you try it."

"Don't mind if I do," Orville said. "I've got a way with women." He took my place on the stool. Elsie turned to watch him and sneezed. When Orville patted her side, Elsie kicked him off the stool. The bucket went over too.

"You have a way with women, all right," I laughed. "Must be your cologne."

"Must be your cologne," Orville mimicked. He got up and brushed himself off.

"Whoa, whoa," Felix said, holding up his hands. "Hate to interrupt another brotherly spat, but I'm outta here." He left to find someone to deliver the flower order to.

I returned the bucket and stool to Elsie's side and tried again. I squeezed until my forearms burned, but for some reason I couldn't get more than a few drops. I climbed out of the stall and joined Orville in the doorway. "Do you think Debra forgot about us?"

"You, maybe," Orville said. "But not me." He sniffed his armpits to check for BO, then smoothed his hair. "She was checking me out."

We waited a little longer, then decided to look for Debra. After wandering through a few buildings, we headed for the office.

"I think that's her voice," Orville said.

He was right.

But when we got there, I wished he was wrong.

Debra the Destroyer

Debra's voice carried through the gap in the back door to the office. We stopped on the porch. Orville looked at me like I should be the one to interrupt, but I shook my head.

"You go in, Mr. Smooth," I told him.

Our standoff allowed us to catch some of what Debra was saying.

"His cologne was so thick. Elsie actually sneezed." Debra laughed. "You should see him. He got all dressed up to milk a cow!" She cracked up at what was said back to her. "You think that's bad, my dad expects me to ride on a float with him. Gross!"

Orville stared down at his shoes. After a long sigh, he walked away.

I waited on the porch, not sure if I should knock or clear my throat. When I heard her say, "loser," and "joke" I left too. If I confronted Debra, that would only prove I was listening in on her conversation. I hurried back to Elsie, but Orville wasn't there. I finally found him in his truck. I told him I'd find Felix so we could leave.

"The sooner the better," Orville said.

Felix turned up at the end of the long building.

"Where have you been?" I asked.

"Researching," Felix said with pride. He told me that since Dooper Dairy had been around so long, he figured it was a good place to dig up information about Harvey. He asked around and was directed to a guy in the equipment shop. "He was in the same class as Harvey. He told me what happened."

"Not more snooping and gossip," I moaned. Seeing Felix's empty hand reminded me of the flower order. "Did you find Mr. Dooper?"

"Um ... no, but I gave the order to Debra." Felix avoided my eyes.

"You're sure?" I asked. "You sound hesitant."

Felix assured me that he gave it to her while she was on the phone. "Now listen to what I learned about Harvey. He got kicked off the float committee when he was in junior high. He used some of the donated materials for himself and they found out."

"They booted him?" I said with surprise.

"Not just booted him," Felix told me. "Suspended him. And while Harvey was out of school, he got in more trouble. Eventually he dropped out."

"No wonder he's grouchy around floats," I said.

"I can't believe he's still around them," Felix added.

"Maybe it's part of his job," I suggested. "He doesn't have a choice so he takes out his anger on us."

We walked to the parking lot, mulling over what we had learned. At the sight of Orville, I told Felix what happened with Debra. Felix handled it well and didn't say a thing the whole way home. Neither did I.

On the day Elsie was to arrive, we gathered in the metal shop building after school. Orville came by too. He acted like he was interested in the float, but spent most of his time watching Clarrisa with the flag team. After getting dumped by Debra, all he could talk about was getting Clarrisa back. So far she wouldn't give him the time of day. Orville leaned against the door frame and set his chin toward the open field. He puffed out his chest and kept flexing and stretching.

"What's wrong with Orville?" Phoebe asked.

I shook my head. "Don't ask."

When Mitch tried on the blueberry hood, all the attention turned to him.

Felix smirked through tight lips. As student leader, I wanted to encourage Mitch, but it was impossible not to laugh. I slapped my hand over my mouth.

Beep. Beep. The truck with Elsie provided the distraction we needed. The driver stopped at the door.

"Where do you want her?" he asked.

I pointed at our float.

He sized it up, rubbed his scruffy chin, then put the truck in park. Clarrisa took a break from helping the flag team and came over. The driver removed a ramp from the bed of the truck and walked Elsie down nice and slow. At the edge of the float, Elsie stopped and wouldn't go any further.

Orville spoke up in a deep voice. "Here. Let me carry her up."

A few kids giggled. Too bad Clarrisa wasn't one of them. She put her finger in her mouth and acted like she would throw up.

The driver settled things by making a clicking sound with his mouth. Elsie tested the ramp, then climbed onto the float and stepped into the corral.

"Milk her twice a day, morning and evening," the driver told us. "Make sure she has water." He dropped off a bale of hay, sack of feed, bucket, and stool. "Debra showed you how, right?"

"Um ... yeah," I said.

He gave me a nod of confidence, then jumped in his truck. "See you at the parade."

Everyone circled Elsie and marveled at her size.

"I bet she weighs a ton," Mitch said, still wearing the blueberry hood.

"A ton? That's nothing," Orville said, trying to impress Clarrisa.

She responded by rolling her eyes and returning to the flag team.

Phoebe patted Elsie. "Hello, Girl. Don't be afraid."

Others took turns petting Elsie. Crusher started bugging me to milk her.

"It's not evening, yet," I pointed out. My last episode with Elsie was still fresh in my mind. "We should give her more time to settle in."

No one bought it.

Mitch gave me a nudge. "Hurry up, she'll burst. Look at that udder."

"Yeah," Stacey added. "Poor thing."

I climbed into the corral with the bucket and stool. I positioned myself beneath Elsie, said a short prayer, and squeezed.

Not a drop. I tried some more. Nothing.

"I thought you had lessons?" Stacey said.

"Yeah, but just one," I said, stalling. I squeezed and pulled. No milk.

Elsie flicked me with her tail.

"She's getting mad," Clarrisa said.

"So am I," I told her.

"I'll do it," Mitch said. "How hard could it be?"

He hopped inside the fence to milk her, but Elsie stepped away. She watched Mitch like he was a wolf.

"That hood scares her," I said. "Take it off."

Mitch tried, but couldn't remove the hood. He yanked and yanked.

Stacey helped. They strained and twisted. Mitch's eyes bugged out.

POP! The hood came loose and kept going. It thumped Elsie's neck. That did it. She went from nervous to berserk. She swung to the side and knocked me off the stool. Then she head-butted the front of the corral. The whole thing went down.

Everyone gasped and jumped back. I rolled out of the way. Elsie stomped around the float and knocked over our giant dairy products.

Elsie thundered down the ramp and headed for the double doors. She trotted outside and crossed the blacktop. At the grass she charged the flag team. Sam waved her flag back and forth while yelling for the girls to move out of the way. Elsie head-butted Sam's red flag and turned around. With the rest of the team on the blacktop, Sam dropped her flag and joined them. We all gathered there, not knowing what to do.

"Watch out!" Harvey ordered. He pushed past us with a rope, half limping, half jogging. As he approached Elsie, he slowed down and talked softly. His voice was smooth and warm. I couldn't believe it. No more gravely edge or anger. Elsie eyed Harvey with suspicion, then ripped up a clump of grass. Harvey limped closer, talking softly. "Easy Girl."

Elsie gave him a last look, then went for seconds on the grass. Harvey slowly tied a rope around her neck, gave her a few pats, then brought her in. He told us he'd milk her and if we knew what was good for us, we'd get back to work.

    We did.

10

Return of the Orville

That night Orville was the last person in the world I wanted to be around. He decided to take his girl problems out on me. "I'm not pulling the float, so forget it."

I told him that he already said he would and we needed him.

"Why should I? First, you mess things up with Clarrisa. Then you let me make a fool of myself in front of Debra. Pull your own float."

"What about Amanda?" I said. "She made you look like a pretty boy, not me."

"I heard that," Amanda said. She came in from the other room and sat next to Orville. She smoothed his hair. "You mean *hunk*. Look at you."

"No way," Orville said. "Clarrisa can't stand to be around me."

"That's because you're not yourself," I said. "You've changed. Look at you."

Orville examined himself quietly, then stood up. He came at me like he would rip me in two.

Me and my big mouth. "I didn't mean—"

"What did you say?" Orville demanded.

"I said, look at you."

"Before that."

I swallowed hard. "Um ... you're not yourself."

Orville grabbed a handful of my shirt. He pulled my face toward his. "That's it!" He dropped me and spun around. "Don't you get it?"

"Get what?" Amanda asked.

"If I want Clarrisa back, the real me has to come back." Orville thumped his chest. "The real me."

"Meaning?" Amanda wanted to know.

Orville didn't answer. He rushed from the family room and headed outside.

"What's up with him?" my dad asked. He and my mom joined us in the family room.

"I think he's going to win Clarrisa back," I said.

Orville returned a half hour later. Dark rings of sweat circled his armpits. His hair stuck out in every direction. He told us he had been running.

Amanda held her nose. "No kidding. You stink."

"Awesome," Orville said. He stuck his nose in his armpit and inhaled. His face beamed with satisfaction. "I'm back. The rugged, natural me. Back."

Amanda raised an eyebrow. "I think you've confused *rugged* and *natural* with *stinky* and *sweaty*."

Orville dropped to the floor and started doing push-ups. "Clarrisa ... " He grunted and lifted. "Will be ... " More push-ups. "Mine."

"Son, what are you talking about?" my dad asked.

Orville stopped exercising long enough to explain his plan. To get Clarrisa back, he had to return to his old self, the one she liked to begin with.

"You mean the gross, disgusting self?" Amanda asked. "The one with grease under your nails?"

"Don't forget hair," I added.

Orville beamed with pride. "Now you got it!"

"No. It can't be," Amanda whimpered. "All my work for nothing." She buried her face in her hands.

I rallied to Orville's defense—not just because I wanted to get on his good side, but because in a way it made sense. Clarrisa did like Orville the way he had been. Even my dad thought the plan had merit. We both asked how we could help.

Orville started with me. "Dig through my dirty clothes and bring me the smelliest you can find."

I held my nose. "On second thought, maybe I don't want to help."

"Maybe you don't need my truck," Orville replied. He knew he had me and shifted to my dad. "Leftover chili. Do we have any?"

"I'm on it," my dad replied. "There's some hidden in the back of the fridge."

"Bring it on," Orville shouted. He raised his arms in victory. Amanda nearly fainted from the BO. I held my breath and stepped back, staring at Orville in awe. The smell of my dad's chili could singe nose hairs. Normally, Orville avoided it at all cost. But not tonight.

I headed upstairs to Orville's bedroom. I couldn't believe how neat it looked. Then I opened his closet. Everything that used to clutter his room was there. I took a deep breath and started digging. I pushed aside sweaty socks and damp towels. I tossed a wrinkled white shirt over my shoulder. Then I saw them. Eureka! A pair of jeans that could stand by themselves. An orange T-shirt stained with grease and mud and wadded into a clump. I tossed both on his bed and ran into the hall just as my air gave out. I looked for Orville downstairs, but he had gone outside. I found him under his truck.

"What are you doing out here?" I asked.

He slid out and stood up. His hands were covered with grease. A drop of motor oil slid down his cheek. That answered it.

"Where are my clothes?" he asked. I told him and he headed back inside. After changing, Orville joined the rest of the family in the kitchen. Amanda had already put a clothespin on her nose. Mom immediately pinched her nostrils. I breathed through my mouth. The stench of his dirty clothes, smelly body, and my dad's chili reminded me of rotten eggs, cow pies, and burnt rubber all mixed together.

"Mom, make him stop," Amanda said with a nasal voice. "We're his family. How will this make *us* look?"

She started to say something to my dad, but he interrupted. "I've added extra garlic and onions, Son, just for you."

Orville sat down at the table. "Bring it on."

My dad removed the bowl of chili from the microwave and brought it to the table. "Dig in."

Orville scooped up a giant spoonful of the steaming red-brown slop. Amanda tried to talk him out of it, but Orville wouldn't listen. He was in a zone. He breathed in and out to psych himself up. My dad watched with pride.

The first bite hit Orville like a sledge hammer. His eyes watered. His jaw tensed. He took another bite, working the chili through his mouth and teeth. He kept going until it was gone. Then he smiled for us. "Clarrisa, here I come."

A fragment of green onion stuck to his upper teeth. A smashed red bean clung to his lower gum.

Amanda covered her eyes. "This isn't happening. I'm a Plummet. He's a Plummet. This can't be happening."

Orville stood. He exhaled long and slow, sharing his breath with all of us. You could practically see it. My mom steadied herself with a chair to keep from fainting.

"Show time," Orville said and rushed out the door.

"Knock her dead," I said after him.

"He will if he breathes on her," my mom added.

Amanda wandered into the family room, mumbling something about changing schools or planets. Mom and Dad stayed in the kitchen to clean up. I did too, wanting to give them an update on the float. We were still there when Orville returned.

"What happened?" I asked.

He sat down at the table. "Her mom said she wasn't home."

My mom pinched the bridge of her nose like she had a headache. "Her mom?" For some reason hearing that was particularly hard for my mom to take.

"Yeah, she came to the door," Orville said. "But she wouldn't let me in."

My mom massaged her temples. "Hmmm, I wonder why?"

I went over and gave Orville a pat on the shoulder. "Clarrisa wasn't there, huh? Her loss."

"Yeah," Orville said with a grin. The red bean and green onion still held like troopers. "Her loss."

The flowers arrived the day before the parade. We were ready for them—barely. It took a while to repair Elsie's damage to the float. We also had to finish testing the Dooper Scooper 2000. Good thing Mr. Dooper was generous with the ice cream. We went through five flavors before it was ready.

Harvey complained about having to milk Elsie twice a day. But when we offered to help, he said we would just mess things up. We could tell he liked taking care of her even though he wouldn't admit it.

Once the flowers were unloaded from the truck, we started gluing them to the giant dairy products. The whole team was in the metal shop building. Stacey looked back and forth between the bundles of flowers and our float. "I love this part!"

She wasn't the only one. Everyone grabbed flowers and took them to their projects. Everything was going great. We had violets for the yogurt, daisies for the hunk of cheese, and roses for the giant can of whipped cream.

I surveyed my team and smiled. So far so good.

Then Phoebe tapped me on the shoulder.

"The carnations are pink," she told me.

I looked at the flower she was holding. "So?"

"They're not white," Phoebe explained. "The only white flowers are roses—and they're for the top of the whipped cream container. We need flowers for the milk bottle. That's Dooper Dairy's main product." Phoebe reminded me that we were supposed to get dozens and dozens of white carnations, not pink ones. White.

"Felix!" I shouted.

"What?" he asked, looking guilty.

I told him what had happened. "You're sure you turned in the exact order we gave you?"

"Um ... yeah," Felix said. "I remembered exactly what we needed."

"What do you mean *remembered*? You had a written list. You didn't need to remember anything."

Felix turned away. He was hiding something, I could tell. "Um ... when I was talking to people about you-know-who, I sort of lost the list. I had to write up a new one."

I slapped my forehead. "Felix! Didn't I tell you to forget about—" I glanced at Harvey's office, "you-know-who. Now look what you've done."

"Sorry. But I know I turned in the right order." Felix looked at the team that had assembled around him. "I'm sure I ordered white carnations."

"Sure you did," I said. "That's why they sent us a truckload of *pink* carnations. Have you ever had a glass of pink milk? Do you remember seeing pink milk in the supermarket? Huh?"

Felix got mad and raised his voice. "Sorry, Mr. Student Leader. I guess I'm not perfect like you." He headed for the door. "Make your own float. I quit—this time for good."

"Oh sure, leave us now—right when it's crunch time." I yelled after Felix but he didn't stop. He didn't turn around. He just kept walking until he was gone. "Not again!" I shouted at no one in particular.

Again.

11

Pick Me

I turned around to a bunch of frowns and crossed arms. Their expressions said I had overreacted, that I was too hard on Felix. Phoebe looked like she would cry. Even Crusher shook his head. A twinge of guilt needled me. But there was nothing I could do. There was no time to chase after Felix and beg him to come back again. We had a float to finish.

I thought of Nehemiah and how he encouraged everyone to build the wall, no matter how many disappointments and setbacks the Israelites faced. The Lord was their courage and strength. They kept at it. So could we. I gave a quick summary of Nehemiah's story. "Come on, you guys. We can't quit now. This is what we've been waiting for. It's glue time!"

No one jumped up and down, but before long they returned to their projects. Stems were clipped from flowers. Flowers were glued to the giant dairy products. Gradually the float improved and so did attitudes.

"What about the pink carnations?" Phoebe asked.

I told her I would call Mr. Dooper and explain the problem. I tapped on the window to Harvey's office and asked to use the phone. Harvey grumbled, but let me in.

Mr. Dooper took the call right away. "How's my float look?"

"Um ... great. It's really coming along." I gave him a quick update, then carefully mentioned the problem. I didn't blame Felix. I just told him there was an order mix-up.

"Pink!" he shouted. "You trying to doop me, Boy? Because nobody doops a Dooper."

I told him that I wasn't.

Mr. Dooper ranted and raved about there being no such thing as pink milk. He was so loud I pulled the phone away from my ear. He told me I had better find a way to fix the problem or else. He was about to hang up when Harvey grabbed the phone. He turned the tables in no time, saying that if Mr. Dooper knew what was good for him he would get us the white carnations pronto. He carried on about how hard we had worked and how Dooper Dairy should be grateful. By the time Harvey was done, Mr. Dooper agreed to call the florist immediately.

Ten minutes later Mr. Dooper's secretary called back saying the flowers would be delivered sometime in the night.

"Awesome," I exclaimed. I started to thank Harvey but he wouldn't let me. He told me to inform the team and get back to work.

The news went over big. We smeared glue on flowers and stuck them to the float, feeling good. It might take a late-nighter, but the float would be finished on time. God had answered our prayers. Everyone was having fun, that is everyone except Orville.

Since his return to slob-dom, he had made no progress with Clarrisa. His big plan ended the night it began. My mom refused to let him leave the house again smelling like a sewer. Orville went back to the way he was before Amanda transformed him, but with far less confidence. He leaned against the float and watched Clarrisa. She was outside with the flag team.

I took a break from gluing flowers to encourage him. "Just take her a rose."

"What for?" Orville asked. "I'm over her. Mind your own business ... or else."

"You're not over her. Take a rose. Quit being such a chic—" I slapped my hand over my mouth. I suddenly realized what *or else* meant. No truck.

"Did you just call me a chicken?" Orville demanded.

I shook my head. I would have said something, but I couldn't. My hand was glued to my mouth.

"What'd you say?" Orville went on.

I answered with "mmm" and he figured out what had happened. He made sure everyone knew.

"You glued your hand to your face?" Stacey squealed. She acted like this was better than a pop quiz. She immediately took advantage of the situation. "Willie, I'm taking a break. I'd like you to finish my project. If that's a problem, speak up. Okay, great. Thanks."

Crusher took his turn. "Willie, here's an idea. I'll eat all the ice cream Dooper donates. If that's not cool, let me know." Crusher turned away so he couldn't see me shaking my head. "I guess that's a yes."

Even Phoebe got in the act. "Elsie's stall is a mess. Cowpie city. The first person with his hand on his mouth gets to clean it up."

That did it. I turned and twisted and ripped my hand loose. "Enough!" With everyone still cracking up I made my way to Harvey's office. He gave me cleaning solvent, and I didn't even care that he grumbled the whole time.

I rejoined the group and expected the teasing to continue, but guilt must have overtaken them. Orville was the first to pat me on the back. "Just kidding, Bro. I should have helped."

Mitch came next. "Sorry, Dude. We were just messing around."

"Yeah," Phoebe added, resting her hand on my back. "That was mean. Are you okay?"

I told them I was fine and that we should get back to work.

"Sounds like a leader to me," Mitch added.

So many apologies and pats followed, I started to think they were overdoing it. Then I noticed that my sweatshirt felt heavy. The front kept sliding up. I pulled it down, but pretty soon the collar was in my throat. I reached back and felt something. Soft. Petals. I twisted and pulled my sweatshirt around. Flowers covered my entire back. I looked like a human float. I found a sheet of paper too. It said, "Pick me."

I glanced up. Everyone was staring at me.

"Get it?" Mitch joked. "Instead of 'kick me,' it says 'pick me.'"

Everyone roared. They bragged about who glued the most flowers to my sweatshirt.

"You can be your own float," Stacey said.

"Think that's funny, huh?" I grabbed a tube of glue and some daisies and chased her down. I managed to glue a few to her back before she retaliated. Pretty soon everyone joined in. Phoebe went after Mitch. Crusher went for Orville. When Clarrisa came in from outside, Stacey pounced with a handful of rose petals. I started for Mitch. We might have gone on for hours, but a loud shout stopped us cold.

"What's going on here?" a grumpy voice wanted to know. It was Harvey, his arms crossed, his face red.

We all froze. No one made a sound ... except a giggle. Orville was trying to glue a daisy to Clarrisa's sleeve. She laughed and pushed him away. When Harvey shouted a second time, they froze too.

We looked at one another, then I couldn't control myself. I smirked. I tried not to, but couldn't help it. Phoebe followed. Pretty soon we were pointing at each other and laughing our heads off. We looked like teenage bouquets.

"What in tarnation?" Harvey grumbled, saying he'd never seen the likes of a group like ours.

I had to hold my sides they hurt so bad.

Harvey glared at us, but something in his face changed. The hard lines faded. His eyes softened just a little. For a moment I thought the impossible might happen, that he might actually smile. But he didn't get the chance.

"BEES!" Phoebe screamed.

A half dozen bees flew in the giant sliding doors. At first I didn't think much of it. They just wanted flowers. Then I realized who the flowers were on.

Us.

"Run for it," Crusher shouted.

We looked like cockroaches in the light. We scurried in every direction. The bees kicked into a frenzy. Their relatives arrived. Dozens poured through the sliding doors.

Orville locked himself in his truck. Phoebe and Clarrisa bolted for the bathroom. Others went for Harvey's office. I just wanted out! I sprinted for the P.E. field.

Sam's flag team was dead ahead. "Sam! Help!"

The flowers on me took Sam buy surprise. She just laughed and pointed. So did the rest of the flag team. Then they realized what was happening. Sam waved her flag at the bees. The team followed her lead.

I finally collapsed on the grass, exhausted. "Are they gone?"

"Looks like it," Sam said.

The team made a few jokes about all the flowers glued to my clothes. Not Sam. She just stared at her flag.

"Thanks for helping me," I said. I asked her how practice was going.

"We had a perfect routine going," she said. "Then you came out."

I told her I was sorry and yanked a rose from my shirt. "Here. This is for you."

Harvey's History

I didn't want to return that night. But I knew that as student leader, I should be the one to sacrifice sleep. Orville drove me to school and stayed. My parents made him. They didn't want me to be alone with Harvey.

As soon as we stepped into the metal shop building, Harvey griped at us to keep it down. Then he disappeared into his office. I let out a sigh and sat down on the edge of the float. All we had to finish was the giant bottle of milk. The rest of the dairy products looked great.

But I still felt cruddy.

Felix was gone for good. My best friend. My right hand man. And he wouldn't be on the float with me. I told myself it was his fault for messing up the order. If it wasn't for him, I'd be at home right now snuggled in bed.

Orville picked up a yellow daisy and plucked off a petal. "She loves me. She loves me not."

Reason number two to be depressed. Orville. I was stuck with a sad, girlfriendless brother for the whole night.

Then there was Harvey, the grumpiest man on earth. No wonder he was kicked off the float as a kid. It's a wonder the flowers didn't wilt when he walked by. Other than Elsie, I doubted he had a friend in the world.

I tried to think about positive things, about how much we had accomplished. But the negatives just kept coming back. What if Debra couldn't control Elsie and she smashed up our float during the parade? I stared outside. Sam came to mind. What if the flag team dropped their flags and tripped over each other?

Bowing my head, I said a prayer. I silently told God everything that was on my mind. When I finished, I heard Orville snoring. He had stretched out on the float. I unzipped my backpack and pulled out my Bible. Maybe another look at Nehemiah would help. Chapter four told how Nehemiah encouraged the people. They worked from dawn until the stars came out. Chapter six said the wall around Jerusalem was completed in 52 days with God's help. Nehemiah denied himself food for the sake of the people. If he did that as their leader, why couldn't I deny myself sleep?

Suddenly my circumstances didn't seem so bad. Compared to Nehemiah I had no right to complain. I went back and forth between reading and praying. The worry and guilt went away. I began to feel at peace. I knew God would take care of me, and the float, and everyone else.

"What ya readin'?" a gruff voice wanted to know.

I looked up. Harvey stood there in denim overalls, his hands deep in his pockets.

I told him that I was reading about Nehemiah and how he handled things as a leader.

Harvey said he'd never cracked a Bible in his life.

"You should," I said. "There's a lot of great stuff in here."

He shrugged, like that may or may not be true.

I told him how the Bible had helped me, especially with all the pressure to build the float. I mentioned the problems we had had and how kids acted like it was my fault.

"Welcome to the club," he muttered.

I thought he would walk away, but he just stood there. Pretty soon, I felt led to ask him a bold question. "Were you really kicked off the float team when you were a kid?"

"Who told you that?" Harvey demanded.

I swallowed. "Someone at Dooper Dairy told Felix."

"Felix, huh? Figures." Harvey limped to his office mumbling something about meddlesome kids. I heard a scraping sound and grunting. A few minutes later he returned with the rusty trap. He shoved it at me, like I should take it.

I didn't.

"I suppose you heard about my Kid Catcher," Harvey snapped.

I sat perfectly still, not sure how to answer.

Harvey grabbed a metal folding chair. He straddled it and turned the trap over in his hands. "When I was in eighth grade, our float recognized the early frontiersmen that settled this area. Kids dressed up in coonskin caps like Davy Crocket. A big company donated fishing and hunting supplies ... like this trap."

"They gave it to you?" I asked.

"Nope. I took it." Harvey explained that when the teachers found out, he was kicked off the float committee and suspended from school. "The only thing this trap ever caught was me."

I looked at his foot then back at the trap. I pictured the steel teeth snapping shut. "That's why you limp, huh? You stepped in the trap."

"Huh? What kind of fool notion ... " Harvey grumbled at me like I was a dope. "It didn't catch my foot. It caught me as a thief. It tempted me and caught me. Get it?"

I nodded.

Harvey turned away. "At first I wouldn't give it back. Then when I tried it was too late." He confessed to getting in more trouble while on suspension and eventually dropping out of school.

I didn't say anything. My mind was busy putting the pieces together. No wonder Harvey was grouchy around floats. He was still dealing with something that happened more than 50 years ago.

A thought came to mind. It felt weird to bring it up, but I had to say something. "It's not too late with God."

Harvey looked at me. "Huh?"

"For God to forgive you," I said. "If you ask Him, He will."

"Why would I?" Harvey muttered. "It wasn't His trap."

"See. That's why you need to read the Bible." My heart was pumping out of my body, but I kept talking. I told Harvey that all sins are committed against God. "That's why we go to Him." I explained that Jesus is the Son of God who died on the cross for our sins. By believing in Jesus as our Savior our sins are forgiven. I opened to John 3:16 and read it.

Harvey listened without saying anything. He glanced at the verse, then stared with intense eyes. "I'll have to think about that." He stood up and went back to his office and closed the door.

I sat there with a tingly feeling. I couldn't believe what just happened, that I had shared my faith with Harvey, the grumpiest man alive, the most feared man on campus. Harvey. I prayed some more. I thanked

God for giving me the words and I asked for Harvey's heart to be opened.

My head was still bowed when the truck arrived. Midnight.

The delivery man rushed in. "You Plummet?"

I told him I was.

Orville stirred from his sleep and Harvey stepped from his office just as the flowers were unloaded. A few big boxes later, we were set. The delivery man shoved a clipboard at me. "Sign here."

He gave me a copy and took off. I got out the glue and scissors. Orville stretched and came over to help. I watched Harvey, thinking he would join us, but he didn't. He went to check on Elsie.

Orville started on one side of the milk bottle. I started on the other. I told him about Harvey while we worked. We clipped stems, glued, and pressed white carnations on the frame of the giant milk bottle. Eventually, Orville started yawning. I struck up a conversation about Clarrisa to keep him awake.

"What's up with you two?" I asked.

"Nothing," he mumbled.

"But you were laughing together. I saw it."

"I know," Orville said with a shrug. "But I asked her to ride in the truck with me and she said she couldn't handle the competition."

"Debra?"

Orville nodded and went on about what a fool he had made of himself.

I told him not to give up, but he wouldn't listen to me. As a last ditch effort, I repeated my earlier idea. Flowers. They were everywhere.

"Make her a bouquet," I said. "When she shows up, give it to her."

"What if she doesn't? Because she won't."

"Then we'll find her. You know she'll go to the parade to see Sam's squad. Instead of stepping from the float to hand out ice cream, I'll give Clarrisa the flowers from you."

Orville checked out all the extra flowers still attached to stems. "You're sure it's okay?"

"They'll be in the dumpster by morning. You might as well use them."

Orville shook his head. "If I spend time on that we'll never finish this float."

I looked at our progress so far. "Yes we will. Take a break to make the bouquet, then help me."

Orville finally agreed and started on the bouquet. I worked faster to make up for him. My progress was good. Two to three hours and we'd be done.

When Orville finished with the bouquet, he asked if a short nap was okay. I told him that was fine. He needed to be alert if he was going to drive in the parade. He stretched out a piece of canvas and curled up. Seconds later his snores filled the metal shop. The low rumble made me sleepy. My work suffered because of it. I got sloppy. I tried to force my eyes open, but couldn't. I decided that a short nap might help me too. I set the alarm on my watch, then curled up in the corral.

The next thing I knew, it was daylight.

You Snooze You Lose

"NO!" I wailed, jumping to my feet. I checked my watch. 9 a.m. The float team was due to arrive at any minute. I roused Orville. "Wake up! Wake up!"

"Huh? What?" he sputtered. He rubbed his eyes and rolled over. "Leave me alone."

"Get up!" I yelled. I turned to look at the giant bottle of milk. "Hurry! Get—"

I stopped shouting. There was no need. White carnations covered the milk bottle from top to bottom. It was finished. Not only that, it looked great.

"I don't believe it," I gawked. "You did it, Orville. You're the man."

"Did what?" he muttered. He sat up and rested his arms on his knees.

"You finished the float," I said, shaking his shoulder. "Awesome."

"Not me," Orville said. "I never budged. Sorry."

"But if you didn't ... " I looked around, thinking someone on the team came early. "Stacey? Mitch? Phoebe?"

No answer.

We both stared at Harvey's office. A garbled snore came from within. "You don't think that ... "

"Must have," Orville said. He stood next to the giant milk bottle. "Nice work, too. Check out how Harvey spelled 'Dooper' with rose petals. Looks like the real thing."

I scratched my head.

Orville brought up my talk with Harvey. "Looks like you got through to him."

I shook my head. "You mean God got through to him." I walked slowly to Harvey's office, filled with disbelief and guilt. So much for the grouchiest, grumpiest custodian in Glenfield Middle School.

I poked my head in the door. Harvey was curled up on the couch, still snoring. I wanted to wake him up and thank him. He didn't have to help us. It wasn't his responsibility. Staying here all night was sacrifice enough. I eased toward him to nudge his elbow, then decided it would be nicer to let him sleep. I'd thank him later. We'd all thank him later.

Orville and I removed the extra flowers and materials from the float. We picked up loose petals, stems, and scissors. I found the flower order and headed for the trash can. On the way I glanced at the list of flowers. The daisies, roses, and violets were all there.

And so were the white carnations.

"White carnations?" I said aloud. I checked the date. They were on the first order along with everything else. Felix got it right. The florist messed up the order, not him. No wonder the flowers were rushed out in the middle of the night. They weren't doing Mr. Dooper a favor. They were making up for their own mistake.

"Me and my big mouth," I grumbled. "Orville, you gotta take me to Felix's."

Orville wouldn't hear of it. "There's no time. Just call him."

I quietly slipped into Harvey's office and dialed Felix's house. It rang. And rang. No one answered. The answering machine clicked on.

I hung up without leaving a message. I ran to the float and kept going. "I have to go get him! Hook up the trailer. I'll be right back."

Orville started to object, but I bolted from the garage. Felix had to know that he didn't mess up. He deserved to ride on the float as much as anyone. I had to get to him. And fast!

I did.

WHAM! I slammed into Felix as I rounded the building. We both tumbled.

"Felix, I can't believe you're here," I said. "I was just—"

Felix rubbed his head. "I know what you're going to say and I'm sorry. I messed up the order. It was my fault. I shouldn't have been—"

"No, you didn't. You got it right!" I showed Felix the purchase order.

He beamed. "What'd I tell you? You wanted white carnations, so I ordered white carnations."

I stood up and extended my hand. He took it and rose to his feet. I apologized for doubting him and being a lousy student leader.

"No, you're not," Felix said. "Some people just make more mistakes than others—and you happen to be one of them."

We laughed and jogged into the metal shop building. Felix climbed on the float and marveled at the finished product. He inhaled and savored the fresh scent of flowers. "Smells as good as it looks."

One by one the rest of the team arrived. We wheeled the trailer around and Orville backed up his truck. Debra pulled up just as we attached the hitch. Her outfit told us there had been a change of plans. She had on a long silver dress, high heels, and make-up.

"You're going to milk Elsie in that?" I asked.

She just rolled her eyes like I was the dumbest kid on earth. "I'm not going to milk Elsie at all. The mayor's wife is sick, so I get to ride with my parents in the grand marshal's carriage." She went on about what a privilege it would be and that I would have to milk Elsie. "You've been doing it anyway, right?"

Before I could tell her otherwise, Debra hurried back to her car and drove away.

The entire team stared at their leader. Me.

"Now what?" Mitch asked.

Crusher crossed him arms. "Without Debra to control Elsie, we're toast."

"We can't take her," Stacey said. "It's too dangerous. She'll have to stay behind."

Orville appeared from behind the float. He had been hiding since Debra pulled up. "No way. Elsie's the center piece. She has to go."

I let out a long sigh and glanced toward Harvey's office.

Orville noticed. "What are you thinking, Bro?"

I could tell he already knew, but wanted me to tell the group. "Harvey."

"Harvey what?" Stacey wanted to know.

I told them about our talk last night, about what happened when Harvey was a kid and how he suffered because of it. I explained that I shared about Jesus and forgiveness. Then I told them more big news. "Harvey finished our float for us. Not Orville. Not me. Harvey."

"No way," Crusher said.

"Way," I replied.

When Orville verified my story, everyone stared at Harvey's office in awe.

That was my cue. I walked to the door and knocked. He grumbled and spoke gibberish. I knocked again. Harvey peeled open an eye. "What'd you want?"

"Um ... we kind of need your help." I told him that Debra backed out and how he was the only one who could milk Elsie and keep her calm.

Harvey sat up and smacked his gums. "What are you gettin' at?"

"We want you to ride on the float with us, Harvey."

"You're crazy." Harvey wouldn't look at me. He started to lay down.

I stepped toward him. "Please, Harvey. We need your help."

Harvey grumbled all the way to his feet. "Let me get this straight. You want me to ride on a float in the Founders' Day Parade. A float from Glenfield Middle School?"

I nodded.

He shook his head. "Nope. Me and floats don't mix. I had my chance."

"That was over 50 years ago. Remember what we talked about last night? Forgiveness. We need your help. Besides, you belong on the float as much as anyone."

"I don't think so." Harvey turned away and fussed with papers on his desk.

"Come on, Harvey. Help us," I pleaded. "At least think about it."

Harvey scanned his office. The ratty old furniture. The refrigerator. The trap.

I walked back to the group and gave them the report. Then I said something that surprised even me. "Let's pray for him."

The kids seemed a little shocked, but they bowed their heads with me. I prayed that Harvey would go along with us and that he would think about what I told him last night. When I said amen we stared at his office. He didn't come out. One by one, we climbed on the float for the final preparations. I was the last one aboard when the door squeaked.

Harvey stood there in his overalls. He held the rusty steel trap in his hand.

No one spoke. Or breathed. We just watched him.

Harvey limped toward us, his steps heavy and slow. The chain attached to the trap jingled. He didn't stop until he was right in front of us.

I swallowed and pulled my eyes from the trap. "Does this mean you're going?"

"You got a lotta nerve, Plummet," Harvey told me. He lifted the trap and chain over the trash can and brought it down with the force of a slam dunk. "Let's go!"

"Yeah!" I started a chant. "Har-vee! Har-vee!"

Others joined in. "Har-vee! Har-vee!"

We circled around him and thanked him for finishing the float.

His response was classic. He grumbled at us to knock it off and get busy. When we hesitated, he raised his voice and said we'd miss the parade if we didn't get a move on. I didn't want to be disrespectful, but it was impossible not to smile. For some reason, getting yelled at never felt so good.

Founders' Day Fiasco

The floats and classic cars, marching bands and horseback riders all held their positions. The sun rose above the buildings. The sweet smell of flowers and stench of livestock mixed and confused our noses. People ran in every direction adding final touches. Then the whistle blew. The first car pulled ahead. I started to sweat. My white milkman costume fit me fine, but I felt funny wearing pants on such a warm day.

Sam and her team were directly behind us. She gave them some last minute advice and kept it positive. When our eyes met, she winked, letting me know she had taken my advice to heart.

Now if only Clarrisa would show up. She was no where to be found. I had the bouquet that Orville made for her laying behind the giant cup of yogurt.

A man wearing a green jacket waved us forward. Orville put the truck in first gear and started off. We

pulled onto the parade route and cruised along Third
Street. Orville kept it nice and easy. Five miles per
hour and steady. Mitch waited inside the giant cup of
fruit yogurt with Stacey. Phoebe peered through a
hole in the Swiss cheese. Harvey sat on a stool next to
Elsie, giving her a gentle pat. Crusher and another kid
stood next to the giant milk bottle.

Crowds lined each side of the street, waving and
clapping. Good thing we were moving. The speed cre-
ated just enough breeze to cool us down.

Sam's flag team marched behind us. They looked
great so far. Flags up, then down, then twirling.

"Ready, Felix?" I asked.

He nodded and flipped the switch. The Dooper
Scooper 2000 came alive. The arm raised. The scoop
pivoted and dug into the bucket of chocolate ice
cream. It raised again, turned, then dropped the ball
of ice cream directly into a cone. Perfect.

I handed the cone to Phoebe. She stepped off the
float and gave it to a kid with a crew cut. He acted like
Phoebe was an angel. "Thanks! Thanks a lot!"

I delivered the next cone myself. Soon we were
the most popular float. Kids waved and asked for ice
cream. There was such a commotion that Mr. Dooper
looked back from the grand marshal's carriage. He
gave me the thumbs up, thrilled that the float with his
name on it was the hit of the parade.

I went back and forth delivering ice cream. So did
Crusher. Stacey and Mitch waved to the crowds,

berry hoods and all. Felix tended the machine and Harvey milked Elsie.

The easiest job went to Orville. I felt bad about Clarrisa, but at least Orville could relax. No shifting, turning, or braking. All he had to do was keep it nice and steady.

Too bad that was easier said than done.

Suddenly, we started to slow down. I looked at Orville. His head leaned back. Way back. Our speed kept decreasing. Sam tried to compensate. She took smaller steps. Her team caught on and copied her. In front of us the grand marshal's carriage pulled away.

"I think he's asleep," Felix said.

Orville's nervous energy had finally given out. With the parade under way and Clarrisa out of sight, Orville was down, drained, and discouraged.

"Do something," Crusher said.

I tried not to panic. I smiled and shouted at the same time. "Orville!"

He didn't budge. We eased to a standstill.

So much for not panicking. "ORVILLE!"

That woke him—and then some. Orville jerked his head forward. His foot must have jerked too because the float shot out from under us.

I reached for something to keep me from falling. Elsie's tail.

"MOO!" Elsie bellowed. She kicked the corral and rammed it with her head. Harvey jumped up and grabbed her harness. The pail of milk tipped over. I let go and fell backward. I landed on the Dooper Scooper 2000.

"NO!" Felix cried out.

By the time I got up, ice cream balls were launching into the air.

Felix adjusted the controls, but it didn't matter. Ice cream pelted the crowd like snowballs. One landed in a woman's hair. Another pegged a kid's arm. Others shot straight for Sam's team. So much for their formation.

"Do something, Felix," I stammered.

"It won't respond," he said. "You broke it."

Harvey clung to Elsie, whispering in her ear. She stepped back and forth, like she would bolt at any minute. We knew the corral wouldn't hold her. Harvey struggled to keep her under control. He limped this way and that. His wrinkled hands stroked her hide.

"Moo!" Elsie let out. She raised her head and flicked her tail.

Felix finally managed to shut down the machine. But the damage was done. The crowd grumbled and pointed. Everyone's attention was on us. Negative attention. We needed something, and fast.

Sam.

I called her name and gave her a desperate look.

She knew what I wanted. She bit her lip. I could tell she was nervous. But that didn't keep her from helping. She nodded and blew her whistle three times. The girls raised their flags. Show time. Their most complicated routine was about to begin.

They took off. Weaving. Angling. Stepping to the side. Crisscrossing. Their flags spun. Twirled. They tossed them in the air. Single rotations. Then doubles. The girls caught their flags perfectly and spun around. They never missed a step or broke formation. It was amazing. When Sam gave the last toss, we watched the flag spread out and rotate three times then land in her hand. Awesome. The crowd thundered with applause. No one cared about us anymore. All eyes were on the flag team. Sam's hard work had paid off.

I clapped as loud as anyone. So did everyone else on the float. We started to breath a little easier. Then we slowed again.

Orville's head bobbed this way and that.

I had to take action. I jumped off the float and went to him. "Orville, wake up!" I ordered. I marched to his door and waved at the crowd.

"I'm okay," Orville told me. He blinked and stretched his face.

I returned to the float knowing he needed help. I prayed for a solution. I scanned the crowd. Then I saw her. Clarrisa. She stood next to a telephone pole just ahead of us. I grabbed the bouquet and rushed to her. Everyone around her gawked and smiled.

"Where's mine?" a woman teased.

Clarrisa blushed. I whispered that the flowers were from Orville and told her what was happening. "Will you help him?"

"Willie!" Clarrisa objected.

I pleaded with her. "Please, Clarrisa. He needs your help."

I left her there to decide. If it wasn't for me, they wouldn't have broken up in the first place. At least I tried to make up for it.

I passed Orville on the way back to the float.

"Thanks, Bro," he said.

Clarrisa didn't move, but the crowd had parted around her. She wouldn't look at Orville or the float. She stared down at the flowers and sniffed them.

The truck grew closer. Closer.

When it pulled along side her, she stuck out her thumb and smiled. "Going my way?"

Orville nodded and grinned from ear to ear.

Clarrisa ran to the passenger door. The crowd loved it. They clapped and smiled and gave Orville the thumbs up.

"If that doesn't work, nothing will," Stacey said.

"Who's ready for ice cream?" Felix asked. He hit the power button.

I squinted, not sure what to expect. The Dooper Scooper 2000 raised its arm, pivoted, dropped, and dug. It strained against the ice-cream, then rose and swung toward the conveyor belt. The ball of ice cream dropped in the middle of the cone.

"Yes!" I hollered. "Back in business."

I gave Felix a high five. Crusher delivered the first cone and Phoebe grabbed the one after that. We served the crowd like before, making kids happy on both sides of the street. As a thank you, I even took a cone to Mr. Dooper. When Debra wanted one, I delivered one to her too.

The parade ended at the park. The judges came along and awarded prizes. We weren't surprised when Sam's team got first out of all the flag teams. We didn't do as well, but considering what we had been through, third place was fine. Everyone thanked me for heading up the project. I apologized to Stacey for the mean things I said about last year's float. She told me she was sorry for setting me up as student leader but liked how things worked out.

When the photographers came around wanting a picture, we posed on the float.

"Wait a minute," I said. "Where's Harvey?"

We found him hiding behind Elsie, totally out of sight. We pulled him around to be in the picture. Harvey fussed and complained with each step, but he stayed where we put him.

I patted his arm. "Harvey, without your help this day wouldn't have been possible."

I waited for him to grumble and grouch and tell me to get back to work. But he didn't. He just swallowed and put his arm on my shoulder. Then the photographer counted to three.

And Harvey smiled.